MULK RAJ ANAND, bor
University of Punjab and at
career by writing for T S Eli
international fame with his neart-warming portraits of the
Indian landscape and its working class. Author of more than
a dozen novels, short stories and critical writings, including
*Untouchable, Coolie, Private Life of an Indian Prince, Seven
Summers, Death of a Hero,* and *Lament on the Death of a Master
of Arts,* he was honoured with Sahitya Akademi Award, the
most prestigious Indian award for literary writing, in 1972.
He has held the Tagore Chair at the Punjab University and
was also the Chairman of Lalit Kala Academy.

'With great deftness, Anand pictures India ...He impresses
with his profound knowledge of Indian religion and
culture.'

Books Abroad, USA

The Lost Child

AND OTHER STORIES

MULK RAJ ANAND

Orient Paperbacks
DELHI | MUMBAI | HYDERABAD

www.orientpaperbacks.com

ISBN 13: 978-81-222-0368-4
ISBN 10: 81-222-0368-X

1st Published 2004
3rd Printing 2010

The Lost Child... and Other Stories

© Mulk Raj Anand, 2004

Cover design by Vision Studio

Published by
Orient Paperbacks
(A Division of Vision Books Pvt. Ltd.)
5A/8, Ansari Road, New Delhi-110 002

Printed in India at
Saurabh Printers Pvt. Ltd., Noida

Cover Printed at
Ravindra Printing Press, Delhi-110 006

Contents

The lost child
. . . and other stories

The Lost Child

Dedicated to Frances Connery-Chappell

*I*t was the festival of spring. From the wintry shades of narrow lanes and alleys emerged a gaily clad humanity, thick as a swarm of bright-coloured rabbits issuing from a warren. They entered the flooded sea of sparkling silver sunshine outside the city gates and sped towards the fair. Some walked, some rode on horses, others sat, being carried in bamboo and bullock carts. One little boy ran between his parent's legs, brimming over with life and laughter. The joyous morning gave greetings and unashamed invitations to all to come away into the fields, full of flowers and songs.

'Come, child, come,' called his parents, as he lagged behind, arrested by the toys in the shops that lined the way.

He hurried towards his parents, his feet obedient to their call, his eyes still lingering on the receding toys. As he came to where they had stopped to wait for him he could not suppress the desire of his heart, even though he well knew the old, cold stare of refusal in their eyes.

'I want that toy,' he pleaded.

His father looked at him red-eyed, in his familiar tyrant's way. His mother, melted by the free spirit of the day, was tender, and giving him her finger to catch, said: 'Look, child, what is before you.'

The faint disgust of the child's unfulfilled desire had hardly been quelled in the heavy, pouting sob of a breath, 'm-o-th-er,' when the pleasure of what was before him filled his eager eyes. They had left the dusty road on which they had walked so far. It wended its wary way circuitously to the north. They had come upon a footpath in a field.

It was a flowering mustard field, pale like melting gold as it swept across miles and miles of even land — a river of yellow liquid light, ebbing and falling with each fresh eddy of wild wind, and straying in places into broad rich tributary streams, yet running in a constant sunny sweep towards the distant mirage of an ocean of silver light. Where it ended, on one side stood a cluster of low, mud-walled houses, thrown into relief by a dense crowd of yellow-robed men and women from which arose a high-pitched sequence of whistling, creaking, squeaking, roaring, humming noises, sweeping across the groves to the blue-throated sky like the weird, strange sound of Siva's mad laughter.

The child looked up to his father and mother, saturated with the shrill joy and wonder of this vast glory, and feeling that they, too, wore the evidence of this pure delight in their faces, he left the footpath and plunged headlong into the field, prancing like a young colt, his small feet timing with the fitful gusts of wind that came rich with the fragrance of more distant fields.

A group of dragon-flies were bustling about on their gaudy purple wings, intercepting the flight of a lone black bee or butterfly in search of sweetness from the flowers. The child followed them in the air with his gaze, till one of them would fold its wings and rest, and he would try to catch it. But it would go fluttering, flapping, up into the air, when he had almost caught it in his hands. One bold black bee, having evaded capture, sought to tempt him by whining round his ear and nearly settled on his lips, when his mother gave a cautionary call: 'Come, child, come on to the footpath.'

He ran towards his parents gaily and walked abreast of them for a while, being, however, soon left behind, attracted by the little insects and worms along the footpath that were teeming out from their hiding-places to enjoy the sunshine.

'Come, child, come,' his parents called from the shade of a grove where they had seated themselves on the edge of a well. He ran towards them.

An old banyan tree outstretched its powerful arms over the blossoming jack and *jaman* and neem and *champak* and scrish and cast its shadows across beds of golden cassis and crimson gulmohur as an old grandmother spreads her skirts over her young ones. But the blushing blossoms freely offered their adoration to the Sun in spite of their protecting chaperon, by half covering themselves, and the sweet perfume of their pollen mingled with the soft, cool breeze that came and went in little puffs, only to be wafted aloft by a stronger breeze.

A shower of young flowers fell upon the child as he entered the grove, and, forgetting his parents, he began to gather the raining petals in his hands. But lo! he heard the cooing of the doves and ran towards his parents shouting: 'The dove! The dove!' The raining petals dropped from his forgotten hands. A curious look was in his parents faces till a koel struck out a note of love and released their pent-up souls.

11

'Come, child, come!' they called to the child, who had now gone running in wild capers round the banyan tree, and gathering him up they took the narrow, winding footpath which led to the fair through the mustard fields.

As they neared the village the child could see many other footpaths full of throngs, converging to the whirlpool of the fair, and felt at once repelled and fascinated by the confusion of the world he was entering.

A sweetmeat seller hawked: 'Gulab-jaman, rasgula, burfi, jalebi,' at the corner of the entrance, and a crowd pressed round his counter at the foot of an architecture of many-coloured sweets, decorated with leaves of silver and gold. The child started open-eyed and his mouth watered for the burfi that was his favourite sweet. 'I want that burfi,' he slowly murmured. But he half knew as he begged that his plea would not be heeded because his parents would say he was greedy. So without waiting for an answer he moved on.

A flower-seller hawked: 'A garland of *gulmohur*, a garland of *gulmohur*.' The child seemed irresistibly drawn by the implacable sweetness of the scents that came floating on the wings of the languid air. He went towards the basket where the flowers lay heaped and half murmured, 'I want that garland.' But he well knew his parents would refuse to buy him those flowers because they would say they were cheap. So without waiting for an answer he moved on.

A man stood holding a pole with yellow, red, green and purple balloons flying from it. The child was simply carried away by the rainbow glory of their silken colours and he was possessed by an overwhelming desire to posses them all. But he well knew his parents would never buy him the balloons because they would say he was too old to play with such toys. So he walked on farther.

A juggler stood playing a flute to a snake which coiled itself in a basket, its head raised in a graceful bend like the neck of a swan, while the music stole into its invisible ears like the gentle rippling of a miniature waterfall. The child went towards the juggler. But knowing his parents had forbidden him to hear such coarse music as the jugglers played, he proceeded farther.

There was a roundabout in full swing. Men, women and children, carried away in a whirling motion, shrieked and cried with dizzy laughter. The child watched them intently going round and round, a pink blush of a smile on his face, his eyes rippling with the same movement, his lips parted in amazement, till he felt that he himself was being carried round. The ring seemed to go fiercely at first, then gradually it began to move less fast. Presently the child, rapt, finger in his mouth, beheld it stop. This time, before his over-powering love for the anticipated sensation of movement had been chilled by the thought of his parents' eternal denial, he made a bold request: 'I want to go on the roundabout, please, father, mother.'

There was no reply. He turned to look at his parents. They were not there, ahead of him. He turned to look on either side. They were not there. He looked behind. There was no sign of them.

A full, deep cry rose within his dry throat and with a sudden jerk of his body he ran from where he stood, crying in red fear, 'Mother, father!' Tears rolled down from his eyes, hot and fierce; his flushed face was convulsed with fear. Panic-stricken, he ran to one side first, then to the other, hither and thither in all directions, knowing not where to go. 'Mother, father!' he wailed! with a moist, shrill breath now, his throat being wet with swallowing his spittle. His yellow turban came untied and his clothes, wet with perspiration, became muddy where the dust had mixed with the sweat of his body. His light frame seemed heavy as a mass of lead.

Having run to and fro in a rage of running for a while he stood defeated, his cries suppressed into sobs. At little distances on the green grass he could see, through his filmy eyes, men and women talking. He tried to look intently among the patches of bright yellow clothes, but there was no sign of his father and mother among these people, who seemed to laugh and talk just for the sake of laughing and talking.

He ran hotly again, this time to a shrine to which people seemed to be crowding. Every little inch of space here was congested with men but he ran through people's legs, his little sob lingering: 'Mother, father!' Near the entrance to the temple, however, the crowd became very thick: men jostled each other, heavy men, with flashing, murderous eyes and hefty shoulders. The poor child struggled to thrust a way between their feet but, knocked to and fro by their brutal movements, he might have been trampled underfoot had he not shrieked at the highest pitch of his voice: 'F-ather, mother!' A man in the surging crowd heard his cry and, stooping with very great difficulty, lifted him up in his arms.

'How did you get here, child? Whose baby are you?' the man asked as he steered clear of the mass. The child wept more bitterly than ever now and only cried: 'I want my mother, I want my father!'

The man tried to soothe him by taking him to the roundabout. 'Will you have a lift on the horse?' he gently asked as he approached the ring. The child's throat tore into a thousand shrill sobs and he only shouted: 'I want my mother, I want my father!'

14

The man headed towards the place where the juggler still played on the flute to the dancing cobra. 'Listen to that nice music, child,' he pleaded. But the child shut his ears with his fingers and shouted his double-pitched strain: 'I want my mother, I want my father!' The man took him near the balloons, thinking the bright colours of the balls would distract the child's attention and quieten him. 'Would you like a rainbow-coloured balloon?' he persuasively asked. The child turned his eyes from the flying balloons and just sobbed: 'I want my mother, I want my father.'

The man, still importunate in his kindly desire to make the child happy, bore him to the gate where the flower-seller sat. 'Look! Can you smell those nice flowers child? Would you like a garland to put round your neck?' The child turned his nose away from the basket and reiterated his sob: 'I want my mother, I want my father.'

Thinking to humour his disconsolate charge by a gift of sweets, the man took him to the counter of the sweet shop. 'What sweets would you like, child?' he asked. The child tuned his face from the sweet shop and only sobbed: 'I want my mother, I want my father.'

15

The Eternal Why

Dedicated to Frances Connery-Chappell

*H*e leaned over the edge of the boat dangling his hands to reach the water, while his mother held him fast by the end of his tunic to prevent him from falling over. It was the central boat of the static fifty-one which supported the wooden bridge that had been built over the River Lunda, because no other could stand its ferocious moods. Today, however, on a sultry afternoon in May, the stream was slow and peaceful. As the child bent over it he could see his silhouette and that of his mother reflected in the imperceptibly moving water.

This reflection of him sitting in the water was a curious phenomenon, something he had never seen before: it might almost have been his first awareness of life. He stared hard at it, from its immediate life-size through its gradual exaggeration to where his mother's form faded in the current and his own attained maturity by being elongated into an oval. Then, suddenly, he looked away as if self-conscious at having looked too much on himself, as if afraid that if he kept on looking he would not be able to resist the fascination of his form in the water.

'Why do we sit here, mother?' he asked, as he settled back into the boat for a moment.

'We are eating the air, child,' his mother replied vaguely, as she sat melting away into her shadow in the stream.

'Why do we eat the air, mother?' asked the child, opening his mouth wonderingly.

'We want to see a bit of life in the evening, my son,' she replied, with a delicately evasive smile.

He turned away, more amazed than satisfied by her answer.

His pure new consciousness was innocent of this aspect of reality — the river and the reflection of his form in its water.

He bent his head to look at it again. The image had now crystallized into a more shapely form and was not merely vague and silent in the distance.

'Mind you don't fall, looking into the river, child,' warned his father from where he sat smiling benevolently on the high stern end of the boat, just as the child's gaze had drifted from his own form to the reflection of the Sun splintered into countless stars upon the moving water.

Vaguely he heard his father's voice and equally vaguely he saw the Sun dancing in the rippling stream. Both the sound of his father's voice and the sight of the Sun's reflection disturbed his attention. He became busy reaching out for the little pieces of wood that came floating on the surface of the river. He would hold these bits of timber in a pile, but as they grew in number some of the pieces would drift away from the assemblage and he would extend his arm to catch

17

them. Some of these he would arrest, others eluded his grasp. But he was not irritated if he failed to catch them and he went on collecting, re-collecting his treasure of chips from the floating blocks. Thus utterly absorbed in his game, he acquired a sort of power to concentrate on all the various moods of the current and cultivated almost the vivacity of the sunbeams that played and commingled with the waves.

Once, however, his hand strained to save at least one little piece of wood, when all those he had collected were let loose by the current, and he nearly jumped out of his mother's lap. She suddenly pulled him back and looked, dumb with apprehension, in her husband's face. Then she turned to the child remonstratingly: 'Child, sit still and play here in the middle of the boat. Don't stray to the sides.'

A little shaken by his mother's sudden pull and angry remonstrance, he struggled out of her grasp and sat in safety on a plank of wood that might have served as the rower's seat before the boat was turned to use to sustain the weight of the bridge. For a moment he was quite still. But his secret springs of energy burst forth again soon. The flush of discouragement fled from his face and a naughty light charged his eyes with bright sparks of gaiety. His lips were covered with a smile. He rose and scanned the bridge which chained the boats across the river. He could see men and women walking across it, some heading straight across, others stopping to look at the river, or stepping into the boats to rest a while from the toil of the journey in the heat of the day; still others struggling to steer their herds of donkeys and goats, loaded with all kinds of goods and chattels, clear of the danger of falling into the river. These latter were big, burly men, ferocious and red, like the robbers his mother had told him about in the fairy story. They beat their beasts of burden brutally with huge sticks, to drive them fast, even though the

18

poor animals were quaking under the weights on their backs. The child was frightened when a group of them passed, shaking the whole wooden structure with the powerful thumping of their heavy feet. It seemed as if the bridge which honest workmen had taken years to build would yield to their heavy, clumsy gait, and then every one would go swirling fast down the stream, shouting and struggling to keep afloat in utter confusion among the frothing waves. The child did not know why this should happen; nor what exact form it would take if it did happen; he was just afraid that it might happen, and in order to escape from this dreadful prospect of the future he looked away towards the hollows in the shore on both sides of the now rising stream.

He could hear the mournful wail of water butting into the rocks and he could see shadowy forms, shapeless bodies and featureless faces appear from a little stretch of even bank and vanish into the stream. He looked more intently and could recognize a few heads floating in the water, but like the dancing shadows that projected themselves from the kikar trees into the shimmering stream, like the cool evanescent breeze that arose from the dim, white mist across the water, like the foam among which they moved happily to and fro, they seemed to the child perplexingly unreal and indistinct.

'What is that, mother?' he asked, bewildered.

'They are the holy men bathing in the river, child,' his mother answered. 'They are swimming.'

'I want to swim, too,' he said, and almost made towards the water.

'No, no,' said his mother, running after him. Bringing him near her, she began to console him: 'You are too small to swim yet. One day, when you are big and strong, you will swim, too, my child. Not till then, because the river is very cruel, and even very strong men are drowned in it.'

His gaze, retreating from the banks, began to probe each corner of the bare wooden structure of the boat. He flew and sat on a plank a yard ahead of the boat. Tempted to run farther he almost knocked his head against a high wooden wall that descended from the bridge. His mother raced after him and brought him back.

'Come, child, play here, near me,' she remonstrated. He was a bit cross with his mother for not letting him go and play as he liked. So he ran towards his father instead of coming back to her lap. This parent's benevolent smile consoled him, and for a little while he waited to find something which would revive his spirits. He soon discovered an interesting sensation, for as he stood near the high stern end of the boat he could hear its nose tear the water sharply. He mounted to his father's lap briskly, almost without aid, and looked towards the direction whence the swelling river came. He could see its vast sheet of rippling power converge into an even smaller chasm of silver light till it lost itself in the dim vaults of steep precipices.

Deep, deep in him, deep in his little soul, he knew there was something beyond the river, some dark force, some mysterious source from which it came.

'Where was the river born, father?' he asked therefore, almost as he might have asked for food, knowing there was such a thing to be had.

'It was born in the Himalayas; my child, from the cold, white snows on the roof of the world.'

'Where did the snow come from on the Himalayas, father?'

'It was formed by the rain which the clouds poured down, child.'

'Where did the clouds come from then?' he asked, like a true little philosopher, greedy to know the last cause of all things.

'They came from the sea, my child, from the boundless, infinite ocean.'

For a moment he was quiet and struggled to fit the mountains, the snow, the clouds, the sea into his dark pre-natal feeling for order; but failing to picture all these things either separately or together, he let his imagination try to assimilate knowledge by another course of reasoning.

'What is the name of the river, father?' he asked, urged by the unformulated theory that everything has its name original and primordial.

'It is called Lunda, my son.'

That answer seemed to satisfy him, and for a moment he sat back quietly.

The river was now in full swing. The subtle rhythm of its earlier hissing flow had given place to the crafty play of babbling waves. A wedge of slow ripples had spread the first flaws in a crystal sheet of indomitable power. Ebbing, falling, mounting, remounting, the terrible serpent poured itself down from the plain, a mighty sweep of opulent majesty, and borrowing the lustre of magnificence from the golden sun, enthroned itself upon the earth a mirthful, usurping Emperor.

The child trembled with fear as he contemplated the roaring hum of the demoniac rushing stream. He looked into his mother's eyes for comfort. There was a tender look of reassurance in her dusky face. So he sat safely in conviction of her supporting love, and in a while even mustered courage to stare into the stream again.

A whirlpool engaged his attention: first a disembodied look, then his searching watchfulness. The revolving water did not seem to move. Why did it not move? He looked and looked, waiting for the pent-up snag to release itself. It would not flow. He stared hard at it. There was a difference, but the dimple in the pool persisted, like the dimple on his mother's face. This mark on the dark, leonine, imperious stream persisted, the mystery of the river's soul, so like the mystery of woman's soul, innocent, simple, yet in the end subtle, mysterious, unknowable, perhaps even capricious. He was beaten by the mystery.

'Why does not the water there flow, father?'

'Because there is a deep, deep pit in it and the water gets lost in it.'

'But why does the other water flow?'

'Because it avoids the deep pits and goes over even land.'

He watched the endless, writhing flow of the stream again. But there was still a part of his intuition to be exorcised from the depths below the depths within him. He contemplated his father's answer to his last question and then fired off another.

'Where does the water go, father?'

'It goes to the sea, my son.'

'But it came from the sea, did it not?'

'Yes, my son, it came from the sea; from the boundless, infinite ocean it came, into that vast ocean will it go.'

'Where is the sea, father?'

'It is on the other side of the world, child.'

A smile of endless light lingered in the eyes of the day. It came upon the earth and played about the child's face like a dim aureole as he sat now in his mother's lap in the joy of his newly gained knowledge. Through the burdensome multiplicity of unending experience, he could see that the mystery of the river's origin, the secret of its journey and the riddle of its destination had some significance for him.

But what it was he did not know. As the golden sunlight faded and the silver moonlight fell on the limitless expanse of water power he asked one last question: 'If the sea is on the other side of the world, father, why is the river on this side?'

'They are really in the same world, child. Only they appear to be separated. The river comes from the sea and goes sweeping incessantly onward to it. But I do not know, child. I cannot go on answering your eternal whys.'

But in the darkness of the swiftly approaching night he ran up the hill, his bright face showing to his fellows the torch-light of the conqueror.

The Conqueror
Dedicated to Frances Connery-Chappell

*T*he blazing sun trembled in a smile on the lips of
the Western horizon, a last smile of melting gold. The
sapphire heavens accepted it with the misty haze of fatherly
sobriety. The dusty body of mother earth seemed like a
flowing river of yellow liquid light seen in an ecstatic trance.
The conic peaks of two dizzy heights rose on the surface of
the plain like two purple nipples full of an azure, scarlet blood.

A group of bright-eyed children stood in the bare
shadow of a pipal tree shooting swift arrows of impetuous
speech, while their bamboo bows were still slung on their
shoulders and their arrows still nestled in their toy quivers.
They were of varying ages, but none older than ten and none
younger than six. And though there were a great many of
them, they all seemed of one mind, if not with regard to all
things, yet with regard to two: one, that the higher peak
before them was the fort about which they were to range
themselves in opposing parties to fight and conquer; two, that
the new arrival, the little child of five who was coming with
them, was not to be allowed to take part in the battle,

because he was too small, had no bow and arrow, might get hurt and thus cause them to be reprimanded by their parents.

The piercing rays of the departing sun touched the child's tender heart and set his warm blood flowing with love for the companions he was approaching. There was in him a secret, innocent impulse for friendliness, such as is primeval and spontaneous in all things nearest to nature and which had now taken in him the form of a vague eagerness at the prospect of company. He was full of enthusiasm for his friends and their sport. But as yet he did not know that they would refuse to let him join them, that the thrill of his anticipated pleasure would fade away into the pale weakness of a sighing despair.

He was still some distance away from his fellows, and although he was hurrying towards them his deep, unquestioning faith in all-will-be-well, confirmed by the fixity of the group under the pipal tree, reassured him in the contemplation of the twilight that spread before him.

Red streaks of burning light infused patches of grey cloud as the extinguished pieces of coal-fire lie in the small thick masses of ashes. The hills looked not unlike the dark edges of an oven gently shading from their lower soft pale to blonde wheat, from rich dark olive to red dark purple and finally to an intense black. The vast plain was now like a silken veil of amethyst with every shrub and tuft of grass a deeper green and every grey mound of stone a richer black.

Someone stirred in the group and led the way towards the foot of the hill fixed upon as the fort to be besiged and conquered.

The child shouted to the beat of a grim premonition: 'Wait, I am coming!' and began to run across the grass and stones. The group of elder boys had all turned their backs upon him. He shouted again, still running. They seemed to be walking away unheeding. He shouted yet again, this time with such desperate force that his throat sounded dry and hoarse. His little body became hot and perspiring as his natural haste gave place to a clumsy rush, till he seemed like a fuming ball of smoke let loose into a furious spurt by some sudden blast of confused wind. He pulled himself up for a moment when he saw that his friends had run away from him.

He had now sensed their trickery and stood looking round for a moment. Then, thoughtless, he ran again as if panic-stricken. In the confusion of this rush his bright-eyed, red-cheeked face seemed to dull into a vaporous greasy surface. Unconscious of himself as of his goal, he ran desperately, furiously, with all the might of his little body. A stone, big, round, immobile, lay under the pipal tree, a challenge to be dodged and respected. But the child had no thought for Siva and he had lost the dodging sense. He stumbled across it, hitting his shin, and fell to one side. A little cry rose from his heart, rich with pain, bringing dewy tears to his eyes.

As he lay, however, for a moment looking at the turquoise sky above him and the hazel earth about, the bleak and dreary sense of failure seemed to desert him. A sudden intuition made him obstinate, and in a while tears stopped half way down his cheeks and his sob died down into a sigh and his cry stopped in his belly and would not rise. He cleared his throat of the choking breath that seemed to linger from the last hoarse shout and stood up.

The boys were at the foot of the hill now, a pack who had lost their common conviction through the dislocation caused by haphazard running. They lingered about with their bows and arrows in separate bands as if they had forgotten how to adjust the one to the other. Broken they looked, a mob with no generals, for the boy who had led the way was fat and clumsy and had lagged behind the others, and the boy who had started the intrigue was trembling.

It seemed they were all afraid that the child would tell on them.

The child had different thoughts. Bravely, with a grim determination, he surveyed the conic peak that he knew they had appointed as the fort to be conquered. It stood tall and elegant as a cypress tree. Its shapely form reminded the child of something he had seen before. He seemed impelled by it to go forward, attracted by something magnetic about it, some mysterious mastery it had over his heart.

He ran towards the foot of the hill, his heart beating a steady tattoo to his feet. His gait was full of power now and the small mounds seemed to aid his progress by their slow rises and falls: at each incline his feet moved with the force derived from the last decline.

'Go back, go back!' the boys shouted as he approached the foot of the hill. He still kept running and did not answer.

'Go back, go back!' they called with weak, disapproving, cautious voices.

But in the darkness of the swiftly approaching night he ran up the hill, his bright face showing to his fellows the torch-light of the conqueror.

The Barber's Trade Union

Dedicated to John Lehmann

*A*mong the makers of modern India, Chandu, the barber boy of our village, has a place which will be denied to him unless I press for the recognition of his contribution to history. Chandu's peculiar claim to recognition rested, to tell the truth, on an exploit of which he did not know the full significance. But then, unlike most great men of India today, he had not very exaggerated notion of his own importance, though he shared with them a certain naive egotism which was sometimes disconcerting and sometimes rather charming.

I knew Chandu ever since the days when he wore a piece of rag in the middle of his naked, distended-bellied body, and when we wallowed together in the mire of the village lanes, playing at soldiering, shopkeeping, or clerking and other little games which we invented for the delectation of our two selves and of our mothers, who alone of all the elders condescended to notice us.

Chandu was my senior by about six months, and he always took the lead in all matters. And I willingly followed, because truly he was a genius at catching wasps, and at pressing the poison out of their tails, at tying their tiny legs to cotton thread and flying them, while I always got stung on the cheeks if I dared to go anywhere near the platform of the village well where these insects settled on the puddles to drink water.

When we grew up he still seemed to me the embodiment of perfection, because he could make and fly paper kites of such intricate design and of such balance as I could never achieve.

To be sure, he was not so good at doing sums at school as I was, perhaps because his father apprenticed him early to the hereditary profession of the barber's caste and sent him out hair-cutting in the village, and he had no time for the home tasks which our schoolmaster gave us. But he was better than I at reciting poetry, any day, for not only did he remember by rote the verses in the text-book, but he could repeat the endless pages of prose in that book so that they seemed like poetry.

My mother resented the fact that Chandu won a scholarship at school while I had to pay fees to be taught. And she constantly dissuaded me from playing with him, saying that Chandu was a low-caste barber's son and that I ought to keep up the status of my caste and class. But whatever innate ideas I had inherited from my forefathers, I certainly hadn't inherited any sense of superiority. Indeed, I was always rather ashamed of the red caste mark which my mother put on my forehead every morning, and of the formalized pattern of the *uchkin**, the tight cotton trouser, the gold-worked shoes and the silk turban in which I dressed; and I longed for the right to wear all the spectacular conglomeration of clothes which Chandu wore — a pair of khaki shorts which the retired *subedar* had

---

* A long coat.

29

given him, a frayed black velvet waistcoat, decorated all over with shell buttons, and a round felt cap which had once belonged to Lalla Hukam Chand, the lawyer of our village.

And I envied Chandu the freedom of movement which he enjoyed after his father died of plague. For then he would do the round of shaving and hair-cutting at the houses of the high-caste notables in the morning, bathe and dress, and then steal a ride to town, six miles away, on the foot-rest of the closed carriage in which Lala Hukam Chand travelled to town.

But Chandu was kind to me. He knew that I was seldom taken to town, and that I had to trudge three weary miles to a secondary school in the big village of Joadiala with the fear of God in my heart, while he had been completely absloved from the ordeal of being flogged by cruel masters as he had left school after his father's death. So he always brought me some gift or other from the town — a paint brush, or gold ink, or white chalk, or a double-edged penknife to sharpen pencils with; and he would entertain me with long merry descriptions of the variety of things he saw in the bazaars of civilization.

He was particularly detailed in his description of the wonderful English styles in clothes which he saw the Sahibs and the lawyers, the chaprasis and the policemen wearing at the District Court, where he had to wait for the journey home at the back of Lala Hukam Chand's phaeton. And, once or twice, he expressed to me a secret wish he had to steal some money from the pitcher where his mother kept the emoluments of his professonal skill, to buy himself a rig-out like that of Kalan Khan, the dentist, who, he said, performed miracles in the town, fitting people with rows of teeth and even new eyes. He described to me the appearance of Kalan Khan, a young man with hair parted on one side,

30

and dressed in a starched shirt, with an ivory collar and bow tie, a black coat and. striped trousers, and a wonderful rubber overcoat and pumps. And he recounted to me the skill with which this magician unpacked an Angrezi leather hand-bag and flourished his shining steel instruments.

Then he asked my advice on the question of whether, as a barber educated to the fifth primary class, he would not look more dignified if he, too, wore a dress in the style of Dr. Kalan Khan, 'for though I am not a highly educated doctor,' he said, 'I learnt how to treat pimples, boils and cuts on people's bodies from my father, who learnt them from his father before him.'

I agreed with his project and encouraged him with the enthusiasm I felt for everything that my hero thought or did.

One day I was thrilled to find Chandu at the door of my house in the morning. He was dressed up in a white turban, a white rubber coat (a little too big for him, but nevertheless very splendid), a pair of pumps in which I could see my face reflected in clear silhouette, and he had a leather bag in his hand. He was setting off on his round and had come to show me how grand he looked in his new rig-out.

'Marvellous!' I said. 'Marvellous!'

And he rushed off towards the house of the landlord, whom he shaved every morning, myself following admiringly behind.

There were not many people in the street at this time. So I alone witnessed the glory of Chandu, dressed up as a doctor, except, of course, that he himself seemed rather self-conscious as he strutted up the street, carefully avoiding the taint of cow-dung cakes which the village women stuck to the walls, and the dirty water which flowed through the drains. But as we entered the home of the landlord we met Devi, the landlord's little son, who clapped his hands with

31

joy and shouted to announce the coming of Chandu, the barber, in a beautiful heroic dress like that of the Padre Sahib of the Mission School.

'Ram! Ram! Ram!' said Bijay Chand, the burly landlord, touching the sacred thread which hung over his ear since he had just been to the lavatory. 'The son of a pig! He is bringing a leather bag of cow-hide into our house and a coat of the marrow of, I don't know, some other animal, and those evil black Angrezi shoes. Get out! Get out! You son of a devil! You will defile my religion. I suppose you have no fear of anyone now that your father is dead!

'But I am wearing the clothes of a Doctor, *Jagirdar* Sahib,' said Chandu.

'Go away you, swine, go away and wear clothes befitting your low status as a barber, and don't let me see you practising any of your new-fangled notions, or else I will have you flogged!'

'But Rai Bijay Chand Sahib!' Chandu appealed.

'Get away! Get away! You useless one!' the landlord shouted. 'Don't come any nearer, or we will have to treat the whole house with the sacred cow-dung to purify it.'

Chandu returned. His face was flusehed. He was completely taken aback. He did not look at me because of the shame he felt at being insulted before me whose hero he knew he was. And he rushed towards the shop of Thanu Ram, the *sahukar**** of the village, who kept a grocer's store at the corner of the lane.

Devi, the landlord's son, had begun to cry at his father's harsh words, and I stopped to quieten him. When I got to the head of the lane I saw the *sahukar* with one end of the scale in which he had been weighing grain lifted in one land,

---

*A rich man or a trader who may also be a money lender.

abusing Chandu in the foulest way. 'You little swine, you go disguising yourself as a clown when you ought to be bearing your responsiblities and looking after your old mother. You go wearing the defiled clothes of the hospital folk! Go, and come back in your own clothes! Then I shall let you cut my hair!' And as he said so he felt for the ritual tuft knot on top of his head.

Chandu looked very crestfallen, and ran in a wild rage past me, as if I had been responsible for these mishaps. And I nearly cried to think that he hated me now just because I belonged to a superior caste.

'Go to Pandit Parmanand!' I shouted after him, 'and tell him that these garments you are wearing are not unclean.'

'*Ho*, so you are in league with him,' said Pandit Paramanand, emerging from the landlord's home, where he had been apparently summoned to discuss this unholy emergency. 'You boys have been spoiled by the school education which you have got. It may be all right for you to wear those things because you are going to be a learned man, but what right has that low-caste boy to such apparel? He has got to touch our beards, our heads and our hands. He is defiled enough by God. Why does he want to become more defiled? You are a high-caste boy. And he is a low-caste devil! He is a rogue!'

Chandu had heard this. He did not look back and ran in a flurry, as if he were set on some purpose which occupied him more than the abuse which had been the cause of his flight.

My mother called to me and said it was time for me to eat and go to school, or I should be late. And she could not resist the temptation to lecture me again about my association with the barber boy.

33

But I was very disturbed about Chandu's fate all day, and, on my way back from school, I called in at the hovel where he lived with his mother.

His mother was well known for a cantankerous old woman, because she, a low-caste woman, dared to see the upper caste people as they never dared to see themselves. She was always very kind to me, though she spoke to me too in a bantering manner, which she had acquired through the suffering and humiliations of sixty-odd years. Turning to me she said: 'Well, you have come, have you, to look for your friend. If your mother knew that you were here she would scratch my eyes out for casting my evil eye on your sweet face. And you, are you as innocent as you look or are you a sneaking little hypocrite like the rest of your lot?'

'Where is Chandu, then, mother?' I said.

'I don't know, son,' she said, now in a sincere simple manner. 'He went up town way and says he earned some money shaving people on the roadside. I don't know what he is up to. I don't think he ought to annoy the clients his father served. He is a child and gets funny notions into his head and they ought not to be angry with him. He is only a boy. You want to see him and go out playing, I suppose. Very well, I will tell him when he comes. He has just gone up the road, I think!'

'All right, mother,' I said, and went home.

Chandu whistled for me that afternoon in the usual code whistle which we had arranged to evade the reproaches of interfering elders that our association often provoked.

'Come for a walk to the bazaar,' he said. 'I want to talk to you.' And hardly had I joined him when he began: 'Do you know, I earned a rupee shaving and hair-cutting near the court this morning. If I hadn't had to come back on the

34

back bar of Hukam Chand's carriage early in the afternoon, I should have earned more. But I am going to teach these orthodox idiots a lesson. I am going on strike. I shall not go to their houses to attend to them. I am going to buy a Japanese bicycle from the gambling son of Lalla Hukam Chand for five rupees, and I shall learn to ride it and I will go to town on it every day. Won't I look grand, riding on a bicycle, with my overcoat, my black leather shoes, and a white turban on my head, specially as there is a peg in front of the two-wheeled carriage for hanging my tool-bag?'

'Yes,' I agreed, greatly thrilled, not because I imagined the glory of Chandu seated on a bicycle, but because I felt myself nearer the goal of my own ambition; since I felt that if Chandu acquired a bicycle he would at least let me ride to town on the elongated bolt at the back wheel or on the front bar, if he didn't let me learn to ride myself and lend me the machine every now and then.

Chandu negotiated the deal about the bicycle with an assurance that seemed to me a revelation of his capacity for business such as I had never suspected in him, from the reckless way he spent his money. And then he said to me in a confidential voice: 'You wait for another day or two. I shall show you something which will make you laugh as you have never laughed before.'

'Tell me now,' I insisted, with an impatience sharpened by the rhythm of the excitement with which the spirit of his adventure filled my being.

'No, you wait,' he said. 'I can only give you a hint at the moment. It is a secret that only a barber can know. Now let me get on with the job of learning to handle this machine. You hold it while I get on it, and I think it will be all right.'

'But,' I said, 'this is not the way to learn to ride a bicycle. My father learned to ride from the peg at the back, and my brother learnt ride by first trying to balance on the pedal.'

'Your father is a top-heavy baboon!' said Chandu. 'And your brother is a long-legged spider.'

'I,' he continued, 'was born, my mother tells me, upside down.'

'All right,' I said. And I held the bicycle for him. But while my gaze concentrated with admiration on the brilliant sheen of the polished bars, I lost my grip and Chandu fell on the other side with a thud, along with the machine.

There were peals of laughter from the shop of the *sahukar*, where several peasants congregated round the figure of the landlord. And then the *sahukar* could be heard shouting: 'Serve you right, you rascally son of the iron age! Break your bones and die, you upstart! You won't come to your senses otherwise!'

Chandu hung his head with shame, and muttered an oath at me, 'You fool, you are no good!' though I had thought that he would grip me by the neck and give me a good thrashing for being the cause of his discomfiture. Then he looked at me, smiled embarrassedly, and said, 'We will see who has the last laugh, I or they.'

'I will hold the machine tightly this time,' I said earnestly, and I picked it up from where it lay.

'Yes, break your bones, you swine,' came the landlord's call.

'Don't you care!' Chandu said to me. 'I will show them.' And he mounted the bicycle as I exerted all my strength to hold it tight. Then he said: 'Let go!'

I released my grip.

He had pressed the pedal with a downwad pressure of his right foot, hard, and, as the wheels revolved, he swayed dangerously to one side. But he had pushed the other pedal now. The machine balanced, inclining to the right a little, so that I saw Chandu lift his rump from the saddle in the most frightening manner. He hung precariously for a moment. His handles wobbled dangerously. He was totterig. At this juncture a mixed noise of laughter and sarcasm arose from the congregation at the shop and I thought that Chandu would come to grief with this confusion, if not on account of his utter incapacity. By a curious miracle, however, Chandu's feet had got into the right rhythm for pedalling and his handle had adjusted itself to his stiff hands, and he rode off with me running behind him, bursting myself with enthusiastic 'Shabashes.'

A half a mile run and he repeated the trick.

Though I was very eager to share the joy of his newly acquired skill, I didn't see Chandu the next day, as I was being taken to see my aunts in Verka, straight from school.

But on the third day he called for me and said that he would show me the joke he had talked of the other day. I followed quickly, asking the while: 'Tell me, what is it all about?'

'Look,' he said, hiding behind the oven of the village potter. 'Do you see the congregation of men in the *sahukar's* shop? Try and see who's there.'

I explored the various faces and, for a moment, I was quite baffled.

'Only the peasants sitting round waiting for the landlord,' I said.

'Look again, idiot,' he said, 'and see. The landlord is there, his long-jawed face dirtied by the white scum of his unshaved beard.'

'Ha! Ha!' I shouted hilariously, struck by the contradiction of the big thick moustache (which I knew the landlord dyed) with the prickly white bush on his jowls. 'Ha! Ha!' I roared, 'a sick lion! He looks seedy!'

'Sh!' warned Chandu. 'Don't make a row! But look at the *sahukar*. He looks like a leper with the brown tinge of tobacco on his walrus moustache which I once used to trim. Now you run past the shop and call 'Beavers, beavers! They can't say anything to you!'

I was too impetuous a disciple of the impish Chandu to wait to deliberate.

'Beavers! Beavers! Beavers!' I shouted as I ran past the shop to the edge of the platform by the banyan tree.

The peasants who were gathered round the shop burst out laughing, as they had apparently been itching to, for they had noticed the strong growths on the elders' faces, though they had not dared to say anything.

'Catch him, catch him, the little rogue!' shouted the *sahukar*. 'He is in league with that barber boy, Chandu!'

But, of course, I had climbed up the banyan tree, from which I jumped on to the wall of the temple and shouted my slogan at the priest.

The rumour about the barber boy's strike spread, and jokes about the unkempt beards of the elders of the village became current in every home. Even those who were of high castes, even the members of the families of the elders, began to giggle with laughter at the shabby appearance of the great ones and made rude remarks about their persons. And it was said that at least the landlord's wife threatened to run away with somebody, because, being younger than her husband by twenty years, she had borne with him as long as he kept himself in trim, but was now disgusted with him beyond the limits of reconciliation.

38

Chandu did good business in town during these days and saved money, even though he bought new clothes and new tools for himself and gave me various presents.

The village elders threatened to have him sent to prison for his offences, and ordered his mother to force him to obey before they committed him to the police for a breach of the peace.

But Chandu's mother had for the first time in her life touched the edge of prosperity, and she told them all what she thought of them in a language even plainer than that in which she had always addressed them.

Then they thought of getting the barber of Verka to come and attend them, and offered him an anna instead of the two pice they had usually paid to Chandu.

Chandu, however, had conceived a new notion this time, newer than those he had ever thought of before. Having seen the shop of Nringan Das, the barber of the town, he had applied his brain to the scheme of opening a shop on the wayside at the head of the bazaar, in partnership with his cousin, the barber of Verka, and with Dhunoo and the other barbers within a range of seven miles from his village. He proposed his new idea to his cousin and Dhunoo and all the other barbers at a special meeting of his craft, and, by that gift of the gab which he had, besides his other qualities of Head and Heart, he convinced them all that it was time that the elders of the village came to them to be shaved rather than that they should dance attendance upon their lords and masters.

'Rajkot District Barber Brothers' Hairdressing and Shaving Saloon' has been followed by many other active trade unions of working men in our parts.

Duty

The midday sun blasts everything in the Indian summer: it scorches the earth till its upper layers crack into a million fissures; it sets fire to the water till the lakes and pools and swamps bubble, evaporate and dry up; it shrivels up the lives of birds, beasts and flowers; it burns into one like red pepper and leaves one gasping for breath with a bulging tongue till one spends one's time looking for some shady spot for even the most precarious shelter.

Mangal Singh, the policeman who had been posted on duty at the point where the branch road from the village of Vadala enters the Mall Road of Chetpur, had taken shelter under the sparse foliage of a *kikar* tree beyond the layers of white dust, after having stood in the sun for five and a half hours since dawn. In a little while sepoy Rahmat-Ullah would come and relieve him, and he felt that he could cool down a little and prepare to go to the barracks.

The sun was penetrating even the leaves of the wayside trees, and there was not much comfort in the humid, airless atmosphere, but after the cracking heat of the open, Mangal felt that this comparative shade was a blessing.

He was not, of course, like the delicate lalas, rich Hindu merchants, who rode out into the gardens early in the morning and withdrew after 'eating' the fresh air at sunrise and never appeared till sunset, sitting in the laps of their wives drinking milk-water or lying sprawled about on the front boards of their shops under the cool air of electric fans... No, he didn't say as they would: 'I go for a *pice* worth of salt, bring me a palanquin.' Nor could he 'quench his thirst by drinking dew.' No, he was proud that he came from strong peasant stock and was a hardy policeman who could rough it: indeed, this police service was not active enough for him and he felt it a pity that he had not become a real sepoy; for there was more pay in the *paltans** and there were better uniforms, also free mufti and free rations. So he had heard after he had put the mark of his thumb down and joined the police force — but once done cannot be undone. And it was the blessing of the Gurus, as there was little chance of earning any extra money in the military; while, apart from the fifteen rupees pay, there were other small sums so long as confectioners continued to mix milk with water and so long as there was a murder or two in the prostitutes' bazaar, and so long as there were respectable lalas who would pay rather than have their names mentioned... Why, even here on point duty in the waste land — 'your own is your own and another's is also yours.' For if the peasants offered tokens of grain and butter and sugar to the *Munshi*** at the customs house, then why not to the police? That skinny little Babu at the octroi post had not the strong arm of the sepoy to protect them when they were being looted by the thugs in the market... He knew. After wisdom the club. If only

* Troops/army.
** A term for accountant in rural India.

41

he had been able to pay a *nazar* to the Tehsildar he would never have lost his land to Seth Jhinda Ram. ...But God's work was well done, men's badly. And, truly, if he had not pressed the limbs of the landlord he would never have got the recommendation to join the police. And you learnt a great deal in the service of the Sarkar. And thee was nothing better than service: no worry, and there was so much *izzat* in it that these very cowardly city folk who laughed at you if you were a peasant joined their hands in obeisance to you if you wielded a truncheon. And the rustics who had no notion of discipline or duty could be made to obey authority with the might of the stave, and if they didn't obey that, the fear of the handcuff — even a daring robber like Barkat Ali could not escape because one could blow the whistle and call the entire police force out. And the Sarkar is truly powerful. Like Alamgir, it leaves no fire in the hearth, nor water in the jar, to bring a man to justice....

He glanced at his dust-covered feet in the regulation shoes of rough cow-hide, even as he congratulated himself on his lucky position as a member of the much-feared police service and wished he had really been in the army, for there the sepoys had boots given to them. His puttees too were old and faded and there was something loose about the khaki uniform with the black belt. The uniform of the army was so tight-fitting. Perhaps the whistle-chain and the truncheon improved this and the red-and-blue turban was nice, but — he lifted his hand to caress the folds of his head-dress and to adjust it, as it was heavy and got soaked with the sweat that flowed from his fuming scalp burdened by long hair on the lower edges...

The sun poured down a flood of fire on the earth, and it seemed as if the desolate fields covered with dense brown thickets and stalks of grass and cacti were crackling like cinders and would soon be reduced to ashes. A partridge hummed in its nest somewhere and a dove cooed from the tree overhead, giving that depth to the shade which fills the air with long, endless silences and with the desolate peace of loneliness.

Mangal Singh drifted a few steps from where he was standing and halted on a spot where the shade was thicker than it was anywhere else under the *kikar* trees. And, blowing a hot breath, he cupped his palms over the knob of his stave and leaned his chin on the knuckles of his joined hands and stood contemplating the scene with half-closed eyes like a dog who rests his muzzle on his front paws and lies in wait for his prey.

Layers of white-sheeted mist floated past his eyes in the sun-soaked fields, the anguish of a thousand heat-singed bushes, while the parched leaves of the hanging boughs of the wayside trees rustled at the touch of a scorching breeze.

One breath, a thousand hopes, they say, and there never comes a day without evening — but it would be very difficult to walk down to the barracks through this terrible heat. And he wished his duty was not up, that someone could fetch his food for him and that he could borrow a charpai from the octroi and go to sleep in the grove of neem trees by the garden of Rais Jagjiwan Das, or sit and talk to the grass-cutter's wife who had breasts like turnips. Only Rahmat-Ullah had an eye on her too, and he was sure to be here, as he preferred the desolate afternoon, thinking that he might get a chance when no one was about.

'I will have to walk back to the lines,' he muttered to himself and yawned. He felt heavy and tired at the prospect and his legs seemed to weaken from the knowlede of the unending trudge of three miles. He shook his head and tried to be alert, but the invisible presence of some overwhelming force seemed to be descending on him and his heavy-lidded eyes were closing against his will. He took a deep breath and made another effort to open his eyes wide through the drowsy stupor of the shade that weighed down from the trees. For a moment his body steadied and his eyes half opened. But how hateful was the glare, and how cruel, how meaningless, was life outside... And what peace, what quiet below the trees, beneath the eyes...

If a God should be standing here he could not help closing his eyes for a minute, he felt; and sleep came creeping into his bones with a whiff of breeze that was like a soft beauty retreating coyly before the thousand glares of the torrid sun which burnt so passionately above the silent fields... The heat seemed to be melting the fat in his head and to be blinding his eyes, and he let himself be seduced by the placid stillness into a trance of half-sleep...

Through sleepy eyes he was conscious of the whispering elements as he dozed, and his body still stood more or less erect, though his head was bent on the kunckles of his hand above the stave, and the corners of his mouth dribbled slightly...

'Shoop...shoop...shoop...' a snake seemed to lash his face at the same time as he saw the soothing vision of a dim city through the stealthy corners of whose lanes he was passing suavely into a house was effaced...

'Shoop...shoop...'

He came to suddenly and saw *thanedar* * Abdul Kerim standing before him, his young face red with anger under the affected Afghan turban, his tall lanky form tight-strethed, a cane in his hand, and his bicycle leaning against his legs...

'Wake up! Wake up, you ox of a Sikh! Is it because it is past twelve that your sense have left you?'

---

* Officer incharge of a police station.

Mangal reeled, then steadied himself, his hands climbing automatically to his turban which had been shaken by the Inspector's onslaught.

'Shoop...shoop,' the cane struck his side again and stung his skin like a hundred scorpions. And a welter of abuse fell upon his ears: '*Bahin chod*, the D.S.P. might have passed, and you are supposed to be on *duty*. Wake up and come to your senses, *madar chod*!'

Quite invlountarily Mangal's right hand left the turban and shot up to his forehead in a salute, and his thick, trembling lips phewed some hot stale breath: 'Huzoor *mai-bap*.'

'You eat the bread of illegality,' the *thandedar* shouted. 'I will be reprimanded and my promotion stopped, you swine!'

And he lifted his cane to strike Mangal again, but the sepoy was shaking with fright so that his stave dropped from his hand.

Mangal bent and picked up his *lathi*.

'Go and be on your point-duty!' ordered the *thanedar* sternly and, putting his foot on the pedal, rode shakily away on his bicycle.

Mangal walked out of the shade, his shins and thighs still trembling and his heart thumping inspite of himself, though he was less afraid than conscience-stricken for neglecting his duty.

The heat of the sun made the skin of his face smart with a sharp pain where the perspiration flowed profusely down his neck. He rubbed his hand across it and felt the sweat tingle like a raw wound.

He shook himself and his head twitched, and he looked about in order to see if anyone had seen him being beaten. He wanted to bear the pain like a man. But his eyes, startled by the suddenness with which they had opened, were full of a boiling liquid that melted into fumes as he raised his head.

His throat was parched dry and he coughed with an effort so that his big brown face above the shaggy beard reddened. Then he paused to spit on the road and felt his legs trembling and shaking more than ever. He twisted his face in the endeavour to control his limbs and lunged forward...

'*Ohe*, may you die, *ohe* asses, *ohe*, may you die,' came a voice from behind him.

As he turned round he saw a herd of donkeys come stampeding up the road in a wild rush, which became wilder as their driver trotted fast behind them in an attempt to keep them from entering the Mall Road at that pace.

For a moment the cloud of dust the herd had raised on the sides of the deeply rutted Vadala Road obscured Mangal's view of the man, but then suddenly he could hear him shouting: '*Ohe*, may you die, asses!'

Mangal ran with his stave upraised in a wild scurry towards the driver of the stampeding donkeys, scattering them helterskelter till some of them cantered more quickly into the Mall and the others turned back and came to a standstill. He caught the driver up before the man had escaped into a ditch by the banana field. And, grinding a half-expressed curse between his teeth, he struck him with his stave hard, hard, harder, so that the blows fell edgewise on a donkey's neck, on the driver's arms, on a donkey's back, on a donkey's head, on the man's legs...

'Oh, forgive, Sarkar, it is not my fault,' the man shouted in an angry, indignant voice while he rubbed his limbs and spread his hands to ward off more blows.

'You, son of a dog,' hissed Mangal as he struck again and again, harder and harder as if he had gone mad, till his stave seemed to ring as a bamboo stick does when it is splitting into shreds.

46

A Confession

I don't know why he had to say it to me. But, after listening to the address of Srijut Bishambar Dayal Bhargava on the achievements of the national renaissance during the last few years, I had to go home with Latif and, on seeing him ostentatiously lift the cloth from the sumptuous supper which his wife had left on the table, I had casually let fall the remark: 'I wonder how many coolies have been vouchsafed the advantages of a fifth meal like this, through the Struggle, or for the matter of that, of a meal at all.'

'You are a cynic,' Latif said, and in a characteristic lawyer's manner sought to defend the lovely food against my aspersions: 'You would not wish to deprive those of us who have the good things of the world of their enjoyment of them when you yourself are really trying to afford the poor the advantages they don't possess. You will produce utter chaos in this world if you do that, and law, authority and religion will all go by the board. As you know, there have always been inequalities in this world; the sheep always want to be led, and they want God as much as

47

bread. So it was in the past, so it is in the present, so it will be in the future.'

'I am probably a prig,' I said, 'I have an awful conscience because I feel that the humiliation of the poor is also my humiliation.'

For a while there was a tension in the atmosphere and we went on eating quietly. It was a delicious meal — rissoles, with pickles of various kinds and dry chapattis to eat, and some French white wine to drink. I was enjoying it immensely and yet trying to restrain myself from betraying this either by word or sign, as I didn't want to show that this was a special occasion, and that never since my return from Europe had I tasted French wine.

'I want to say something to you,' Latif began suddenly, dropping his knife and fork. And as I looked up at him, his face was flushed with a certain agitation and his eyes bent down.

'Go ahead,' I said. 'What is it?' And, perhaps because I pronounced those words rather indifferently, Latif hesitated for a moment, looked at me furtively, as if to make sure that I wouldn't laugh at him, and then, leaving his food, burst out quickly, earnestly, in English, as if he wanted to get it over in a mouthful:

'I want to confess something to you. It is sincere. I didn't realize it till now. Honestly! You know I have been a Municipal Commissioner for some years, and this and my practice leave me very little time even to say prayers...I am lucky to have met such an esteemed person as you. In fact, I wrote to my brother in Delhi and told him that you were gracing our house with a visit. So you will realize that it wasn't my fault altogether...'

He paused for a moment. I didn't know what all this rigmarole was about. I was slightly embarrassed by his kindly references to me. But what was he getting at? I made a vague guess or two as to what he was going to say, but before my speculations had taken any shape he resumed his narrative, with the same terrific hurry to get it over with which he had begun.

'I was going up to argue the Habib-ud-Din murder case, the appeal for which was to come up before Mr. Justice Thakur Das at eleven-thirty this morning, and having missed the frontier mail at eight because that *bahin chod, sala* coachman of mine didn't wake me, I reached Lahore by an ordinary train at eleven...'

Something seemed to get stuck in his throat at this and he coughed noisily and, leaning over his chair, spat into the verandah decorated by palms and evergreens. Then, twisting the muscles of his face with anger at the interruption, he began hoarsely:

'I must see the Hakim about this *bahin chod* cough...but I am always so busy, honestly!... You know what a big station Lahore is. The train came into the platform number twelve after its usual slow crawl; it becomes slow like an ant from Mughalpura cantonment to Lahore junction. And there was such a crowd of those uncouth, cumbersome peasants and third-class passengers, struggling to rush up the bridges, knocking your sides about with their staves and their bundles and their bedsteads, you know, I shouted for a coolie to come and bear my suitcase and take me by some less crowded way to the exit near the first-, second- and inter-class booking-office in the hall where I could get a tonga.

49

'The man, a dingy little *poorbia** with a shrivelled face, looked cunning. I didn't like him from the beginning, as he kept very dumb, but he must have been clever; for though he pretended to be a fool, he made a mysterious sign for me to follow...'

Saying this, Latif shook his head and lifted the lid of his left eye, as if to emphasize his estimate of the men's suspicious character, smiled while he paused to create a deliberate suspense, and went on:

'Obviously he had made a practice of smuggling gentlemen who travel *without* out of the station, because he took me through the kitchen of the first-class restaurant, through an assistant stationmaster's office on platform number twelve, across the rails by the steaming engine of the Karachi express, through a soldiers' canteen, and then by a short cut over an empty bridge on to platform number one. He must have been a rogue, as he looked surprised when I took out my ticket to hand over to the ticket-collector at the gate. I am convinced that this coolie imagined me to be *without* as he was almost walking through the doors of the goods godown of his own accord when I called him and directed him towards the proper exit. I am sure he had made a habit of smuggling people for a little bakhshish. Honestly! There could be no doubt about that, but...'

At this Latif saw that my glance was averted from him, and he paused, perhaps because he felt apprehensive that he was not carrying me along with him.

'And then?' I said, affecting an indifferent manner.

'I hailed a tonga when I got outside, but the tongawallah was insolent and, seeing that I wanted only a single seat,

---

* A colloquial Hindi word for individuals born and brought up in Bihar and adjoining areas of Uttar Pradesh.

beckoned a family of five who were waiting for a conveyance. On seeing this, my coolie ran and fetched another tonga for me without my asking him, a thing which made me very angry because I knew that he would want an extra tip for doing that. These railway coolies are pukka badmashes. He put my briefcase into the tonga and, without salaaming or anything, hurriedly stretched his hand out and said: *"Huzoor."*

"*Acha*, be patient, I am not running away," I told him, as the man's abruptness irritated me. I felt that if it weren't for his knowledge of the intricate ways of the station I could easily have borne my briefcase, and I felt that he hadn't earned his wages... As you will admit, a small case isn't heavy... And I couldn't help hating the man for his insolence as he stood. Baba, whatever you may say, these people have raised their heads to the skies and, because they have no breeding, they are absolutely insulting. This man had a sullen expression on his face, and preened himself, thought he was an ugly *poorbia*, because he had twisted his white mustachios, discoloured an orange-red by tobacco on the ends, upright, and had a perfectly clean shave even though his jaws were ugly and hollow...'

I was going to interupt Latif by saying that the fact that the man had a shave and had put out his hand without undue ceremony didn't necessarily mean that he was insolent, but I had hardly opened my mouth when he lifted his hand and raced on eagerly.

'I did not mind, really. I put my hand into the pocket of my *patloon* for the small change I had. I could feel an eight-*anna** bit and four *anna* bits. I took the two nickel

---

* The currency prevalent in India till late 1950s. The pice was the coin of lowest denomination, with four pice making one anna, and sixteen annas making one ruppee.

anna pieces out of my pocket and gave them to him with · a smile, admonishing him jokingly: 'You must give up your illegal traffic in smuggling people without tickets across the station.' But the damn *sala* said curtly, '*Huzoor*, the rate of bearing a case is four *annas*.'

"You are barking an untruth," I said, as his insolence made me very angry indeed. You will admit that the provocation he was offering me was great, particularly as I was in a hurry and he knew he was delaying me. I admit that I was wrong in losing my temper and talking to him impatiently, but I assure you I tried to be as reasonable as I could, and I said to him in a gentlemanly way: "*Bai,* accept what you have been given and don't make a row." But he caught of me, not in supplication, mind you, but to prevent me from going. So you see that I was justified in thinking he was a rogue. "Accept what you have been given," I said, "or I shall hand you over to the police for carrying on that illegal traffic in conveying people without tickets across the station."

"*Huzoor*, *huzoor*, give me my dues," he insisted, bending and joining his hands. Perhaps I was harsh on him, but I didn't believe him when he said: "I don't want anything more than my wages." particularly as he began to insult me openly, saying: "Most people give me a tip, but you look like a *kanjus* Sahib, so I shall be content if you give me my wages."

'I was enraged at his calling me a miser Sahib, as anyone might be on being spoken to like that by a mere labourer. But I was getting late for the Court, and, controlling my anger, I began to board the tonga, feeling that if I had had more time perhaps I would have bargained with him and paid him a little more, as, sincerely, I didn't want to deprive him of his just dues. But he held me back by the lapels of my coat and whined: "*Huzoor*, *huzoor*!"

'I was so annoyed by the touch of the *sala's* dirty hands preventing me from getting on the carriage... You see he was being impudent and impertinent, and I might have fallen, the way he pulled me, as I had one foot on the foot-rest. Then I lost my temper. I descended, and, turning round, gave him a kick so that he fell back weeping. I am sorry I did that, but, sincerely, what else could anyone have done?'

Latif paused as if he had finished his narrative, and he looked at me at once guiltily and as if he wanted to enlist my sympathy for his righteousness and honesty. My face was set without a flicker and yet he must have seen that I considered him blameworthy. He lowered his voice and sought to unburden himself more humbly.

'Some people gathered round to see what was up, and I saw a policeman approaching. It seemed to me a disgrace that I, a respectable citizen, a Municipal Commissioner and a *vakil**, should get involved in an unpleasant scene like that, particularly as I don't like being in a crowd: I get an awful feeling of claustrophobia when I am surrounded — it makes me feel very nervy. So, for a moment, I thought of putting my hand in my pocket and flinging another two *annas* at him, to have done with it all. But frankly, I was keeping two annas to pay the tongawallah, and I wanted to economize, because when you live to a certain standard, you see, you have all kinds of expenses to meet, particularly if you have a large faimily to keep. And I didn't want to change a rupee. And then something very awkward happened: a voice called: "What is the matter, Latif?" and I recognized the face of Gulshan Rai, who is an advocate of the High Court, Lahore, and a friend of mine since college days.

---

* A lawyer.

"*Huzoor*, I bore the Sahib's case from the platform number twelve to hall, and the rate is four *annas*, while the Sahib has only given me two annas," that coolie blurted out before I could say a word.

'I felt utterly humiliated in the eyes of Gulshan Rai and my anger knew no bounds, but I couldn't do anything. Although I would have felt very sorry before you, as it is below my dignity to have been involved in that tow, I could have kicked that *badmash*, I only said to Gulshan: "This man is a fraud." And, sincerely, whatever may have happened, I still believe that he was what I say he was. I told everyone: "I think this man helps people without tickets to get out of the station, and I won't pay him a pice more."

"Oh, come," said Gulshan, "pay him two *annas* more."

'At that I thought of saving my face before Gulshan, as I knew the story would spread in the Bar room and my prestige might be damaged, and I pretended to look in my pockets for change and got out a rupee. I don't often do that. Sincerely. Please believe me. In fact, people will tell you that I am very generous, as I certainly have given more garden parties in this municipality than any other respectable citizen. I don't know what you will think of me. But I did that. And perhaps I am to blame. I don't know what possessed me but I did that.'

His face reddened and he looked very excited, his words now hurtling one over the other.

"I have got two *annas*," Gulshan said. "Don't change the rupee." And he threw the two *annas* at the coolie, saying: "Now run away, my friend, and don't make any fuss. The Sahib is in a hurry."

'I wish I had done to the man what Gulshan did at the very start, and there wouldn't have been any unpleasantness,

54

but I was boiling with fury. "Go now and get out of my sight, otherwise I shall hand you over to the police," I said.

'Gulshan was also going to the Court and he shared the tonga with me, and, though I insisted on paying the fare, he said I had no change and he paid at the end of the journey.'

After saying this, Latif laughed, a half-embarrassed, half-real chuckle. Then he became silent and sat with his head bent down shamefacedly, glancing at me from the pupils of his eyes and opening his lips as if to ask me something, to ask my opinion, my verdict on this affair. And I felt that he expected me to be kind to him and yet admonish him exactly as he had himself done while narrating the incident, now being kind to himself and justifying his behaviour, now admitting his guilt. But there was a pause as I was too embarrassed to say anything. At length, with an effort that made his words tremble, he broke the silence and burst out almost hysterically:

'I couldn't argue my case in Court. My words seemed to get stuck in my throat like jagged-edged knives, and my mind kept forgetting the points. I was so confused...

'And now, I don't know, but I can see that coolie arise from behind my head before my eyes, his blood-streaked eyes, bending over his joined hands, crying and whining and protesting like a black wasp into my ear, whining...

'And at times today I have felt he was following me about. Ugly monolith of a man. Threatening me. With his outstretched, demoniac claws. Threatening me. Threatening me. Just threatening. A dirty, uncouth creature! Threatening me...'

Lullaby

Dedicated to Iqbal Singh

'Sleep
Oh sleep
My baby, sleep
Oh, do not weep,
Sleep
Like a fairy...'

Sang Phalini as she rocked her little one-year-old Suraj Mukhi in her lap, while she fed the machine with handfuls of jute.

Would he ever get to sleep?

'Sleep
Oh, sleep
My baby, sleep...'

His flesh was so warm. She could feel the heat of his little limbs on her thighs, a burning heat which was mixed with a sour smell. He must be ill. All day he had not shut his eyes, all day he had sobbed and cried.

The engine chuk-chuked; the leather belt khupp-khupped; the bolts jig-jigged; the plugs tik-tikked; the whole floor shook like the hard wooden seat of a railway train.

And she had to go on feeding the gaping mouth of the machine. '*Bap re bap*, why is this bitch barking?' the sharp-tongued woman who sang folk-songs, and could brook no one else singing, called to the other women.

'Sleep,
Oh, sleep...'

Phalini felt her throat growing hoarse with the jute fluff she had been swallowing since she had let the fold of the apron rag, with which she ordinarily padded her mouth and nose in the factory, fall loose. The fluff seemed to be everywhere — on the walls, over the machine, on her face. She could feel it streaming down her nose, her cheeks, to the silver ring round her neck which was green with sweat. She cast her eyes over her nose and felt how ugly it was as it stood out from her hollow cheeks. That is why she had pawned her big silver nose-ring which her mother-in-law had given her in the dowry, and refused to adorn her nostrils even though it was a bad omen to take off your jewellery.

'Ooon...ooon...ooon...' Suraj Mukhi cried. The sharp, feeble cry stirred the black night of Phalini's soul as the air stirs the water, but the child's voice was drowned in the dithyrambic hum of the preparing-shed in the factory.

'Sleep
Oh, sleep
My baby, sleep,
Oh, do not weep,
Sleep,'

she sang, bending over the child's head till she almost touched the feverish brow and kissed the close-fisted hands which Suraj Mukhi was rubbing on his eyes, even as he cried. And then she threw another handful of jute into the jaws of the monster.

Her own voice sounded to her like the whisper of a broken reed, completely out of tune today, as it had seldom been out of tune when she sang the work song:

'Roller
Roll
Spread jute
Open mouth,
Rise jute
Fall seeds,
Work into cloth.'

Her big troubled eyes roved away from the child to the gaping mouth of the machine, beyond the black, greasy bolts and knobs and pistons, above the fumes of the thick, sickly, tasteless air in the shed.

The engine chuk-chuked; the leather belt khupp-khupped; the bolts jig-jigged; the plugs tik-tikked; the whole floor shook like the hard wooden seat of a railway train.

She felt giddy.

She had felt like that five months before she had given birth to a child: an oily taste in the mouth with a bile under the tongue that seemed to go quivering into the swollen pitcher of her belly and bring the entrails up to her throat. But the quickening under her navel and the memory of her lover's face seemed to offset the nausea. She tried to think of him now, as he had looked when he first came down from the Northern hills.

The wild, wispish boy with large brown eyes which had flashed when he had talked to her husband, Kirodhar, but which were so shy when he looked at her. Suraj Mukhi's eyes were like his. Also Suraj Mukhi's limbs smelt like his. But he would never know that he was the father of the child. Why, he was a child himself. He had come like lightning and gone like the thunder of the Northern hills...

Where had he gone, she wondered. Had he only come to give her the pang of parting? Where had he gone? It was now summer again and he was here last summer. For days she had scanned the horizon of the sky above the city, towards the north in the direction where he had gone. But he didn't seem to be anywhere in the large breathless space. Only Suraj Mukhi lay in her arms. And the sun, after which she had named the child, stood high. And the tears rolled down her scalded face to her chin, across her cheeks, before she realized that she was weeping... Oh, where was he, the gay child, her lover, her baby, so simple, so stubborn, so strong?

'And I shall grow old and grief, not Kirodhar, shall be my Lord...'

'Ooom...Ooom...' the child moaned.

The engine chuk-chuked; the leather belt khupp-khupped; the bolts jig-jigged; the plugs tik-tikked; the whole floor shook like the hard wooden seat of a railway train. And she had to go on feeding the mouth of the machine.

'*Bap re bap*, what is the matter with the brat? Can't you keep him quiet?' said the woman next to her. Phalini saw him as she had seen him in a dream one day, standing by her side, smiling to her so that she had wanted to clasp him close to her breast. But she had stretched her arms towards him, she had suddenly wakened and found herself groping in the dark towards Kirodhar, who had thought she wanted

59

him and had taken her. He must be somewhere in the far-off hills, doing what?... Wandering perhaps, happy and free, while she was caged here with his child.

She bent down to look at the child. His eyes were open, his face was still, he cried no more. That was good, she could feed the machine with more jute.

> 'Sleep
> Oh, sleep
> My baby, sleep...'

she sang, and she smiled at him and rocked him again. Suraj Mukhi's eyes just stared at her; rigid and hard his little hand lay on the side.

She swayed on her haunches and left the jute.

The effigy lay still.

Dead.

She gave a long, piercing shriek which tore through the ceiling.

She slapped her cheeks and beat her palms on her breast, crying in a weird, hollow voice: '*Hai, hai.*'

'*Bap-re-bap*, why is she crying, this bitch? What is the matter with her?' said the woman next to her.

'My child, my child, my child...' Phalini cried, crazed and agonized as she tore her hair.

The women crowded round her.

'What is the matter?' the forewoman called. 'Why are you bitches running amok?'

The engine chuk-chuked; the leather belt khupp-khupped; the bolts jig-jigged; the plugs tik-tikked; the whole floor shook like the hard wooden seat of a railway train...

The Terrorist

Dedicated to Herring and Oswell Blakeston

*H*e casually presented the slip to the sallow-faced English Inspector of Police who stood at the entrance of the Legislative Assembly buildings in New Delhi. He was making an histrionic attempt to look perfectly unsuspicious and ordinary. He pretended to be lost in admiration of the colossal pillared and domed sepulchre of Sir Edwin Lutyens' architectural dreams without knowing anything about the laws of architecture. He thought that the pretence would work.

But there was an uncontrollable tremor on his lips.

Lest the Inspector of Police notice him pursing his lips tight and lest his bent head arouse suspicion, he brazenly stared straight at the policeman and deliberately waited in that position.

'ADMIT SARDAR BIR SINGH TO THE PUBLIC GALLERY OF THE INDIAN LEGISLATIVE ASSEMBLY' the ticket read in his mind's eye, and he recalled the childish handwriting in which the signature of Rai Bahadur Sir Gopal Chand was sprawled underneath.

Nobody could find fault with that card. He could not have got a more authoritative guarantor than the Deputy President of the Legislative Assembly. 'And I feel I look perfectly calm,' he said to reassure himself.

All this went throught his mind in a flash.

'All right,' said Captain Beatty, alertly looking up to Singh with his hard blue eyes and noticing not the slight tremor on his lips nor the surreptitious manner in which he had lifted his chin, but the face without a blemish; a handsome, wheat-blonde face, with a forehead, shadowed by a khaki polo topee, inflamed by pink-white cheeks, which tapered from the edges of the sharp nose over a regular, expressive mouth down to the chin, whose determination was sadly flawed by the pit of a dimple. 'A Kashmiri pundit, presumably,' Beatty thought, 'a relative of Sir Gopal Chand or a rich university student.' And he dismissed him from his mind because, except that the boy was handsomer than most, he seemed to Beatty like all the other 'native' students who crowded into the public gallery of the Chamber to hear debates, dressed in Ranken & Co. suits and expensive polo topees; such as he himself could not afford on account of those infernal Whiteway Laidlaw bills for Dorothy's dresses which literally poured in by every mail from Bombay.

'I hope that Vasu Dev has got in without any difficulty,' Singh said to himself as he walked up the carpeted stairs and approached the gallery. And he looked past the roped gangway, over the heads of the people who had already taken their seats on his left and right. 'Vasu Dev, Vasu Dev...no...no...yes...there was Vasu Dev...looking...yes...yes, quite unconcerned...there, on the lift in the front row, Shabash! Bravo!'

A light negative shock of electricity passed through his body as he felt for the bomb in the pocket of the overcoat hanging on his arm.

He felt faint.

There was the positive impact of the hand-grenade in the pocket.

He recovered his balance.

He had forgotten to take off his hat, as is the European custom on entering the room. He immediately did so, a little flustered that he might have been noticed with it on all that time. In order to offset any critical gaze that might have noticed him he walked on, looking straight on his right with a hard, impenetrable glint in his eyes, as if that were his usual manner of looking at the world.

There was no seat in the front row on the right, except at the extreme end.

'Stupid,' he muttered to himself, 'that is the fruit of being late. If my coat brushes against any of these fools who have come like dogs to hear the old old debates again under the new reforms, the vessel will be broken. I had better pass through the empty seats at the top and get to the edge of the gallery that way.'

He retraced a step, turned right, and walked quickly but carefully past the folded seats. His feet felt marvellously active, his head was clear and light, though his face seemed covered with perspiration.

As he sat down ostentatiously he was afraid of the bomb exploding on his thighs. He caressed his coat lovingly and, putting it down before him gently, drew his trousers to a comfortable fold above his knees. He had never been very keen on preserving a faultless crease.

63

To avoid the squinting gaze of the man next to him —
a Muhammadan with a red fez, frock coat and baggy
trousers — he looked into the distance on the left and
wondered if he would be able to see Vasu Dev, and whether
Vasu Dev would be able to see him, to time the actual
throwing of the bombs by signs.

He could not discover Vasu Dev at first glance. He
withdrew his eyes. He dared not look left too actively at
once. 'Not yet,' he said to himself. 'I will settle down first
and behave as an ordinary visitor.'

He simulated the manner of an eager young man who
had come to the Assembly Chamber for the first time in his
life, looking as if fascinated at the fake classical frescoes
which decorated the lunettes under the Gothic-Mughal-
American arches of the vast dome of the Assembly building.

The tempera paintings, executed on a background of
gold, described the Hindu seven ages of man: birth, childhood,
student life, love, family life, work, renunciation. The decorative
floral details surrounding the hieratic medallions did not please
him. The unhappiness, the grief, the suffering of all those
phases of life which he had seen in the country about him had
given a sardonic twist to his thin lower lip, and his eyes looked
on at things contemptuously lest his romantic heart illumine
them to the beauty of the world, to the joy of life.

But in a large hemisphere before him on the wall under
the dome he saw the picture of the Buddha preaching to his
disciples. The endless hours during which he had sat at the
feet of the Yogis and ascetics in the various religious shrines,
when he had to live in disguise after he looted the Calcutta
Mail at Kakori and there was a price of a thousand rupees
on his head, and after he had raided the Chittagong armoury,
came to his mind. They had taught him the great doctrine of

securing release from the trammels of existence exactly as did the Buddha. They had pointed a way beyond suffering, beyond the essential unavoidable abomination of suffering. They had described to him the beauty of death. And now he was going to realize that beauty. Only, they had said that one should wait for the culmination patiently. He differed from them there. Death in action, death for such a noble cause as fighting for the honour of the motherland; that was a glorious death. Even according to the enthusiastic Hindus who believed in being born again and again to bear the oppressive sorrows of life from birth to death, one achieved a greater rebirth by doing great deeds. And Guru Gobind and a hundred other saints of his own religion, Sikhism, had achieved martyrdom by fighting against foreign rule. 'Shanti, Shanti,' Peace, the holy men used to say, and truly the Buddha in that picture looked the very embodiment of peace; but, he wondered, had the Buddha known the glory of sacrifice in war? Those communists were right when they talked of revolution, but why did they believe they would become immortal on earth when all religions have taught that immortality is to be achieved only in heaven? Theirs was the militant optimism of materialists and sensualists. They believed that suffering was not inevitable, that they could end it. But they would only conquer the whole world and lose their own souls. No. Death is the only way of securing release from the trammels of existence. All things end in death. 'If India had been free I would liked to have waited for death in peace. As it is, I must die in battle. And the battle is going to rage now.'

His gaze fell on the red plush of the curtains on the tall doors of the Chamber with the hated symbol of the British crown embroidered on them in gold. 'Those curtains are the colour of blood, blood when it has dried,' he said, with a malice born of revenge, which seemed to find a morbid delight in the mysticism of blood, in the pure joy of violence, destruction, and annihilation. 'I wonder if they were deliberately chosen to be of that colour by the government which has won India by the sword and wants to keep it by the sword, chosen by my enemies who believe in bloodshed as I do. Well, soon I shall dye this whole Chamber in the colour of blood. That will be a fit answer to the insolence of these British!'

He felt the blood rise in his veins and colour his face with the wild flush of pride at these thoughts, the flush of pride and power and glory.

He recalled that he had experienced this feeling always at the most critical times in the short history of his life when he was about to kill someone or commit a robbery. He had felt it, for instance, before he shot one of the most prominent police officials at Lahore, and when he had exhorted the crowd at Sholapur to avenge themselves on the British by an open insurrection. It was a beautiful feeling, subtle and warm, like the intoxication of wine. It made one confident and strong...

The thud of awkward feet shambling down into the empty rows of the gallery, the shifting and shuffling of those who were already seated and made room for the newcomers peevishly or with exaggerated courtesy, disturbed his thoughts and annoyed him.

'Fools!' he muttered, 'fools!' And he tried to ignore them by looking around.

A row of scarlet-complexioned Englishmen in frock coats, white shirts and those 'handkerchief' ties (with the pearl pins) which he had never been able to tie, were coming into the distinguished visitors' gallery, with their wives and daughters, looking superior in silver-fox furs. 'No Indians?' his heart asked, 'no Indians among them?' 'No Indians there,' his eyes brought back the answer. His soul rose in a fit of indignation at the insult he thought implicit in this. 'Why are there no Indians in the distinguished visitors' gallery?' he asked. 'Aren't there any Indians left who can defend their honour against such insults? They should make it a point to be there, even if only to keep up the prestige of India before these red-faced monkeys. Surely they are allowed to go in there.'

In the press gallery, beyond the distinguished visitors' gallery, however, he could see two Indians seated beside an Englishman. That was gratifying. 'Though, of course,' he said to himself, 'they must be representatives of the Associated Press of India, which is an English organization.'

A stream of politicians was entering the Chamber past the head chaprasi of the Assembly, whose flowing grey beard wagged over the golden braid of his long red coat every time he greeted a celebrity.

'Fools! Fools! They let themselves be hoodwinked into believing that they now control the destiny of their country,' he muttered. 'They are just like buffaloes and bullocks, the bloated idiots with bored faces!'

He hated them with a hatred of youth's fire against middle-aged indifference.

'Fools! Fools! Bigger fools, those Swarajists! Even they have been taken in by the British.' He fumed inside himself to see some of the sombrely clad members of the Swaraj Party shaking hands with Sir James Ferguson, the Home Secretary, with cordial smiles on their lips. 'Time servers!' he said. 'Opportunists! They only joined the Congress because they wanted to get into the Assembly and to get jobs for their relatives! Traitors!' His feverish eyes explored the faces of the Dishonourable Members even against his will.

There, there was that black Madrasi lawyer and traitor, Law Member of the Government of India, Sir Krishnaswami Iyer, in his small child's turban, embroidered with gold, and a tight, illfitting navy-blue suit, looking more like a scavenging crow than ever with his long, polished nose.

And there, entering the door, was that rich Parsi traitor, Sir Dadiji Maneckji Bottlewala, in English morning dress and a pointed French beard — typical member of the community which fancies itself more English than the English.

'Traitors! Traitors!' he muttered in disgust. 'Traitors! I wish I could blow them up at once. But wait till they have arranged themselves! I will upset them!'

His eyes fell on the beautiful white face of Lala Dwarka Prashad Sharar, the leader of the Congress Party, the folds of whose homespun tunic and loin-cloth fell gracefully on his body like those of the Roman statues in the Lahore Museum. He admired that man. He would have liked to have been like him. He would have liked to have been his son so that he could have inherited the mantle of that distinction which raised the lala to the eminence of a virtual symbol of India. He recalled the occasion when he had first heard the great man speak at the Calcutta Congress. What an orator! The periods of his speech still rang in his ears. The fire of his incitements had sent him raiding, looting, killing, to revenge the wrongs of India. A member of the official nominated party had come to speak to the lala. Singh withdrew his eyes in disgust at the fool who dared to brush up against his hero.

'I must get ready,' he said to himself.

Before feeling for the bomb in the pocket of his overcoat, however, he leaned over the balustrade before him.

The Chamber was now full, above him, below him, about him.

There was a noise of indistinct talk going on, almost like a blurred whisper, punctuated by chatter.

The atmosphere was congested and warm.

He took a deep breath as if he were suffocating. It seemed to make him shiver.

'It is cold,' he tried to assure himself. 'I must soon get active. Then I shall get warm. I had better try and get ready to signal to Vasu Dev.'

He looked towards the left gallery.

The visitors in the public gallery were craning over the red plush of the balustrade and obstructed his view. He could not see Vasu Dev.

He retreated into himself.

A curious emptiness had taken possession of him. It seemed as if he had ceased to exist. But his face was hot and swollen. His ears felt like red, transparent hot iron. His eyes seemed full of molten lava. He tried to pull himself together and to concentrate on the deed.

He had no capacity for abstract thought left, however. The deed that he was going to perform presented itself to him only as a fact in history, in his own chequered history. It was an incident in his life, the last, final incident in his spectacular career, the act which would crown all his efforts at revolt.

Below, everything seemed ready for the Speaker to come in. He waited anxiouly to watch old Mr. Jay Dass Hartal take the chair. 'One of the bravest Indian politicians!' he said in his mind. 'His position as the first Indian President of the Assembly, won after arduous debate, is a glorious victory for the motherland.' He recalled that the sage had blessed him at the Cawnpore* Congress. 'I wonder if he knew that I believed in shedding blood,' he asked himself. 'Still, he was kind to me, even though he had the liberal's horror of taking life. It would be a pity if he were killed when I drop the bomb. But he is old anyway. And I will try to throw the grenade near the official benches.'

No more thoughts came into his head for a moment.

He stared blankly into the air.

Then his glance fell on his knees strongly planted before him, between which lay the overcoat, in the pocket of which was the bomb. His knees began to shake a little.

He diverted his eyes to scan the texture of his overcoat. It was a plain tweed and not stimulating to thought.

He felt as if his head were made of wood which had suddenly become impenetrable to the air.

He shook himself with a slight, hesitant movement of his body and felt as if he were trembling.

Feeling that people about him might become aware of what was going on inside him, he bent his head and looked into his mind's eye.

He felt as if he were shut off from the rest of the world in a dark chamber, alone, a speck of darkness.

But then he became conscious of the presences about him, above all, below him. It was comforting though oppressive.

He wished he could throw the bomb and be done with it.

He suddenly caught Vasu Dev's eyes.

The unbearded young college boy looked wild and furtive, disturbed yet somehow convincing enough. Yes, he could be depended upon. Had he not drunk water out of

*Now Kanpur

the same cup — the symbol of the bitter poison of death? Had he not vowed undying eternal brotherhood and devotion to him, his leader, the liberator of India?

Singh struck the palm of his right hand against his heart and, with his gesture and the movement of his eyelids upwards to heaven, tried to communicate that he loved him and that they were to trust in God above on high and do the right — throw the bombs soon.

It occurred to him in a flash that he had forgotten about the challenge he had intended to utter when he threw the bomb. 'The Challenge! The Challenge!' he said. 'The words which will spread throughout the length and breadth of India like wildfire, words as memorable as those of Proudhon and Mazzini: "I die for my motherland. I become a sacrifice for it. I have tried to avenge *Bharat Mata* against the devilry of the British!" He exulted to think that tomorrow these words of his speech would form the headlines of all the newspapers in Hindustan. He had printed the words on leaflets, so that if all died in the Chamber the printed matter would remain. He felt for the papers in the right breast-pocket of his jacket. They were sa...

The Speaker entered, his long, flowing beard giving a prophetic dignity to his English wig and gown made of homespun cotton material.

The House rose with a rustle.

The Speaker took his seat on the high, throne-like chair.

The members sat down, shuffling, hustling, bustling, talking, whispering.

For a moment all was still again.

Singh saw, or imagined he saw, the three English ministers at the head of the official benches smiling dersively at the ceremonious looks on the faces of the Indian members, as if they who had created democracy could afford to laugh at the mock heroics of these natives whom they were educating in the methods of debate.

He frowned with resentment at so subtle an insult and nearly pulled out the handkerchief from his cuff to wave to Vasu Dev, which act was the signal for the bombs to be thrown simultaneously.

He tried to calm down, to control himself, to go about the business clearly, coolly, deliberately.

But he could not get over the insult implicit in the derisive smile of the English ministers. He felt hot with exasperation, fumed with rage. The memories of the insults which he had suffered at the hands of the British seemed to come back to him.

His eyes dimed with a vague emotion which he did not really feel. He tried to work himself into a towering rage. But his throat seemed parched. He did not know if he would be able to utter the words of his speech when the time came.

The Speaker struck the bell on the desk.

Singh started. His legs seemed to sink beneath him. His heart throbbed violently. His body was perspiring.

He hurriedly put his hand into the pocket of the overcoat and drew out the bomb wrapped in a silken handkerchief.

His heart drummed against his chest now. His temples palpitated. His brain felt dizzy. The words of the challenge seemed to slip through his mind.

He hastily drew the printed leaflets out of his pocket.

His hands were shaking.

He breathed a deep breath, opened his eyes wide, tightened his muscles and prepared to rise.

The Speaker rose.

Singh rose too.

Before the Speaker's eyes had lifted their lids, Singh had flourished the silken handkerchief like a juggler, swept a glance at the Chamber, and thrown the bomb into the air.

'Shoon shut!' The bomb fell at the feet of Sir Arthur Rank, the Finance Minister.

'*Hai*!' Singh heard a cry like Vasu Dev's.

He looked and saw that the boy had been arrested by those about him with the live bomb still in his hand.

'Ooof! Oh, Heavens! We are dead! Undone!' The cries rose from the Chamber and there was complete pandemonium, the cowardly members rushing from their seats and falling over each other, the braver men standing away from their seats.

'Cowards! I become a sacifice for the mother...' Singh shouted.

The old president called the members to order. But his gaze had soared to the public gallery where two men were being held by several others.

Singh's eyes were blurred by the blood that had risen in them. Fire burned in his brain, the fire of strength. Fire swirled in his body as he struggled to wrest himself from the grasp of the policemen about him. He was blind with blood.

A sharp slap fell on his face.

His eyes opened and he faced Beatty.

Tinkle! Tinkle! The President rang the bell and called: 'Gentlemen! Gentlemen! The bomb did not explode! Please return!'

'Oh, what evil stars have robbed my instrument of its power!' roared Singh, writhing histrionically.

'*Bahin chod*! *Suar ka bacha*! *Hosh karo*!' shouted Beatty, again striking Singh's face.

Singh turned his other cheek deliberately, histrionically simulating the appearance of Christ on the cross, and shouted: 'If they hit you on the right cheek, turn your left...'

The visitors in the public gallery who had fled when they heard the bomb drop now came crowding round to see the terrorist, with horror-struck eyes and pale faces. As Beatty and two English police sergeants goaed Singh up the stairs with the butt ends of their revolvers he smiled at the visitors, an automatic smile with a willed patriotism behind it. But for all its patriotism it was a ridiculous smile, the smile of a man who puffed his cheeks when he meant to twist his lips, the smile of a youth who had been suddenly paralysed by fear.

'I sacrifice myself for...' he roared, but the roar ended in a hoarse whisper.

The policeman dug into his ribs and pushed him forward.

'I...' he struggled to say with all the force of his voice.

The word sounded hollow as it struck the dome of the Chamber.

The Interview

Dedicated to Dr. and Mrs. Hussain Zaheer

*I*t was visitors' day at Faridpur Jail.

But, presumably, because Khan Bahadur Sheikh Ahmed Din, the Head Jailer, charged an exorbitant fee, very few people had been able to buy the privilege of a little affection that day. And only three persons waited outside the giant gate with the iron bars for interviews.

One of them was an old peasant, who sat with a load of parcels suspended from a stave which he held across his shoulder. The other was a young woman whose white silk sari fell loosely back from her hair and disclosed a sombre, wheat-blonde face which seemed suddenly tense, for, ordinarily, it would not have shown the slightest trace of self-consciousness, as there was still a twinkle of brightness in the big, brown eyes, even though they seemed to have seen too much. And there was myself.

I remember that I was struck by the contrast between the presence of the weather-beaten, rugged old peasant and this seemingly sophisticated specimen of Indian women of the

75

cities, who change their saris as often as they change their minds and are prone to sit around like dressed-up dolls in badly furnished drawing-rooms, eating betel-leaf galore and occasionally abusing their servants into alacrity. For though, as I came up by the District Courts, where small sleek lawyers flocked around large angular peasants, I could have imagined the old man visiting jail because he seemed poor and obviously had a relation residing in the only place where the poor are most welcome, I could not have fancied this young woman here. Inspite of the fact that I had come to see Ajit Kumar Sen, who had been languishing in Faridpur Jail without a trial for the past two years with group of politicals who had been transferred from the Deoli internment camp, jail was still connected in my mind with criminals, thieves and murderers, with none of whom I could connect this silk-saried young lady.

As I sat down to wait through the hours it takes for the officers of His Majesty's Government in India to negotiate business of any kind, I was made more intensely aware of her presence by my own curiosity, as well as by the attention which the long-mustached, armed warder was paying her; for he stood, rifle in hand, over our heads and fidgeted about, now stamping his feet, now clearing his throat noisily, now striking the butt end of his rifle on the ground, all obviously to attract her attention.

'*Ari*, at least look this side,' he half coughed and whispered in the surreptitious manner of a naïve young heart-squanderer in the market of love who is still respectable enough not to want to be seen in search of a woman too openly.

The woman moved the cloth on her head, shifted on her seat, fanned her face with an edge of her sari and casually shifted her eyes from one side to the other.

Whereupon the warder took a few steps away from her as if he was going to resume his duty as the sentinel of a hell

76

in which the July sun was pouring down the terrible fury of its afternoon hate. But then he walked back and, affecting to inhale a mouthful of breath, heaved a deep sigh, twisted his long mustachios, as though to restore his pride and take the pallor of chagrin off his face.

Some new convicts were coming up the road behind us from the direction of the District Courts, their iron fetters clanking against their chains as they marched; but as yet there was no sign of Sen beyond the iron gates, in the hall. So I interested myself in the antics of the warder.

Unable to recover his equanimity and conscious, perhaps, that the old peasant and I had seen him make vague overtures to the lady, he sought to cover up his desire by humming a love-tune sung by Miss Dulari. But they say, 'Can you cure a heartache by changing the pillow?' and from the lack of confidence in his handling of the melody he seemed to be aware of the fact that he had not much of a voice.

The failure of this approach made him resort to indirect speech again.

'Listeners never hear their praise,' he said to the pock-marked Head Warder, who sat near the small entrance in the giant iron gate, on a tall stool by a high desk, a bunch of keys on a huge ring in his left hand as he wrote on a register propped up before him with the right.

At that the pock-marked Head Warder shouted significantly: 'Why! What's the talk? Today our jail seems to have become a fair. The Moon of Id seems to have arisen on the horizon...' And though his oblique speech referred to the woman, he pointed towards the fresh convicts.

'It is better to be a free bird than a king in prison,' murmured the old peasant, half to himself and half to me as he came to from a moment's doze.

77

The light-heartedness of the Head Warder and the stir in the air produced by the clanking of the new convicts' fetters encouraged the sentry to believe that his open solicitations might expose him to censure.

'*Are*, say a word, O Moon of Id, that I may break my fast,' he said loudly. 'I am dying of thirst.'

The woman turned to me and said, 'Do you think we will be granted the interview soon?'

The warder began to sing a verse about rivals before I could answer her. 'I think the time given was half-past two,' I said.

'It is a quarter to four,' she said, looking at her wrist-watch.

'The Khan Bahadur is probably enjoying his siesta,' I ventured.

'This is their way,' the old peasant said, wiping the sweat off his brow with his hand as he lifted his head from where he had sunk it hopelessly in the pit of his interlocked arms. 'Alas for him whose lawyer has become plaintiff...' And he was burr-burring all to himself when the Head Warder came to the small door, applied a key to the lock, pushed the bars, and beckoned to the policeman in charge of the new convicts to enter.

The clanking of the convicts' chains and fetters as they slowly straggled into the hall ahead of the policeman filled the atmosphere again. But when the group had passed behind the bars and sat down by the Head Warder's desk and the old peasant had relapsed into his stupor, the sentry sensed that his 'beloved' was seeking protection in the shadow of my presence and resumed his steps.

'It took me the whole morning to get a special letter from the Parliamentary Secretary to the Home Minister to enable me to interview Ajit Kumar Sen,' I said, 'now it is taking me the whole afternoon.'

'Oh, I am here to see him too,' she said impetuously, her big eyes lighting up. And a smile of pride seemed to come over her face and she modestly drew the end of the sari on to her head.

'What blandishments! What charm! What to say of Lady Beautiful!' mocked the warder from a distance.

And the old peasant snored as sleep pressed on his eyes.

And the chains and fetters of the new convicts clanked as they shifted for comfort where they sat in the hall.

And I gasped for breath as I looked at the woman and away from her, wondering why, knowing that a woman is open to the lewd jokes of policemen, she had come unattended. Then I contemplated the riveted edges of the convicts' fetters as some of them were bandaging their ankles with wisps of cloth and straw.

'I hear they can get books now,' the woman said. 'And papers. And they have planted a bed of flowers, in the shape of a Red Star with the hammer and sickle on it, inside their barracks.'

'Don't they fear the wrath of authority?' I said, and wondered how they could get space to grow flowers in the overcrowded Faridpur Jail.

'There were some among them who were tied to slabs of ice and paralysed,' she said. 'And others who were tortured...'

'I hear they pierced pins under the nails of some of the students in the camps,' I said. She shook her head and twisted her face and closed her eyes as if not to think of the torture.

'Send the new convicts in one by one,' shouted *Munshi* Dina Nath as he poked his head out of his office on one side of the hall, his tuft-knot dangling a little.

'*Eh Daroga Sahib!*'* I shouted, thinking to catch him before he disappeared forever.

'Oh, are the visitors still waiting,' he said, with an air of shocked innocence. And he came out of his room shouting at the Head Warder: 'Why did you not remind me that these worthy people are waiting?'

'*Huzoor*, we were waiting for orders,' said the pock-marked Head Warder. 'I had the political called and ready for the interview; he is just beyond the door, there in the courtyard.'

'Call him into the hall then! Call him here — into this room — Minister Sahib would be angry if he knew that we had kept a representative of the press waiting. And that lady has a special permit.'

The Head Warder hastened towards the inner wooden gate with his keys and, opening the small aperture, he shouted to a convict warder: 'Sultan, bring the political!'

Ajit Kumar Sen had apparently been seated by the inner door waiting for official sanction. The Head Warder opened the door to admit the prisoner into the hall.

The woman got up from where she crouched and proceeded towards the bars of the outer gate. Her eyes were glued to the sunken-cheeked figure of Ajit, who stood dressed in the fantastic jail tunic and shorts, as he came into the hall.

After the impact of the first strangeness which I felt at not being able to recognize in the stooping prisoner the robust and healthy man I once knew, I waved a greeting.

The warder came up and opened the door in the gate to admit us.

For a moment I waited, partly to look at the old peasant, who still sat neglected where he was under the scanty shade of a sapling near the gate, and to give the woman time to enter.

_____
* Sub-inspector of police.

80

But she stood staring ahead of her.

'*Aiai*, come in!' Munshi Dina Nath said. And the Head Warder looked up with all the eyes in his pock-marked face, expectant and obedient.

The woman lowered her eyes from Ajit Kumar Sen's gnarled face and, bending awkwardly, dragged her feet over the doorstep and scurried like a duck into the hall.

But she had hardly gone two, three steps when she stopped as if to collect herself, stretched her hands, lifted her head and stared at Ajit again, her face set in a mould like a bronze, except that her nostrils dilated perceptibly and her cheeks burned with a quivering flame which transfigured her person.

I had entered the hall and stood behind her.

Ajit stood away, rather distant and inert. The whites of his eyes were vague and liquid in the hollows of the deep sockets. The parchment of his face seemed to have contracted and shrivelled, though he seemed calm and invulnerable in the pride of his position as a prisoner.

The Assistant Jailer went rushing round giving orders to the men in his office to clear out of the way.

The Head Warder stood panting and breathless and scanned the faces of the convicts as if he wished they would scatter.

'*Are*, who do you want to see, oldie?' the warder outside the gate said to the peasant, now solicitous for his welfare.

'Strange that Satan should reprove Sin,' said the old man.

As we stood in the comparative cool of the Assistant Jailer's room I wondered what ties bound Ajit to the woman — what was he to her and she to him?

But, below my nose, her eyes were open and staring, like those of the blind whose eyes never shut, blind as life, blind as death, blind as love...

A Kashmir Idyll
Dedicated to Trilochan Singh and Saeed Hassan

*I*t was during a brief visit to Kashmir, that the incident I am going to relate, took place. But neither time nor space has blurred the deep impression it made on me then, and it has haunted me for many days, so that I must need put it down.

There were originally four of us in the party including myself, the three others being a tall, imposing Sikh gentleman, both tailor-made and God-made; a sensitive young poet, a Kashmiri whose family had emigrated to the plains and made good as Kashmiris always do when once they have left the land where, though nature is kind and generous, man has for centuries most foully and cruelly oppressed man; and a hill boy who cooked for us.

We had loaded our luggage on a tonga and walked the three hundred and seventy-five miles on the road from Jammu across the Himalayas in slow stages, by the beds of the silent Ravi and the surging Chenab. On the peak of the Banihal we had held conversation with the wind that comes from the Kashmir valley, bearing a load of loveliness and pain, the golden exhalation of the saffron and the white sighs of a people who toil unrewarded.

We had descended to the natural spring of Ver Nag from which a few drops of water trickle into a stream that becomes the River Jhelum at Islamabad, where it divides the whole valley into two halves and flows into Lake Wullar and then cuts its way through two hundred miles of mountains into the plains.

From Ver Nag, a village of dark and labyrinthine streets full of small mud huts, the multi-coloured flowers on whose roofs give no hint of the misery which dwells within, we had traversed the main valley by a dusty road bordered by cubist poplars and cypresses.

We had made our headquarters in a houseboat at Srinagar. Then, taking the advice of a tourist's guide book which the government of His Highness, the Maharaja of Kashmir had designed specifically for the use of English visitors, though a few Indians also took advantage of it if they had a smattering of the wonderful, official language, we had decided to undertake short trips to the remote valleys and the unspoiled outlying ranges of the Himalayas within the borders of Kashmir.

We visited the Sonamarg valley where the scarlet eyes of the morning are blinded by the glare of the snow that lies perpetually on the mountain peaks, leading through the Zogila Pass to Chotta Tibet, and where the sleep of the night is continually disturbed by the growling of the angry Indus rushing through glaciers and across high rocks and boulders on its tortuous passage across the Punjab.

We pushed by a difficult track across a crumbling mountain to the cave of Amarnath, where the dripping of water from melting crystals form, a snow image of the shape of a phallus, which the superstitious and the believers go to worship in thousands at a particular time of the year, believing it to be the penis of the Great God Shiva.

We went to Gulmarg, the valley of wild roses; to Lilanmarg, where the lilies of the field grow for miles and miles and miles, angelic and melancholy. We ascended to Aparwat, the high peak above Gulmarg, on top of which is a crystal-clear pool that echoes back the faintest whisper.

We saw Gandarbal and Hari Parbat, the Shalimar and the Nishat; we went everywhere, devouring the beauty of Kashmir's landscapes, trudging along its byways, loitering among its stars, squandering whole days and weeks in search of exquisite moments.

And then there was nothing left to do except to sail among the waterways of the valley, to seek new harbours for our houseboat in the Dal lake and in the shadows of the various gardens, wherever the caprice of our idle wills directed the heart-shaped oars of our boatmen.

A cousin of the poet of our company, a nobleman and courtier of His Highness, the Maharaja, who had sought us out in an obscure corner of the Dal, and showered the blessings of fruit and meat and drink upon us with a generosity that betokened his eminence and his affluence, offered us the hospitality of an island he possessed nearby.

Though grateful for his kindness, we had been finding the gentleman's hospitality rather embarrassing, because it involved us in a friendship with the great man which we could not spontaneously accept. For His Grace was rather a silly young man with the manners of a lout and a high blood pressure in his too opulent flesh, so we excused ourselves by saying that we were intending soon to complete our tour of the valley by going in our kitchen-boat to the Wullar. But

84

it was not so easy for us to escape from the tentacles that he spread around us by that slick and sure turn of phrase that had so obviously carried him to his high position at Court. He suggested that if we didn't accept his hospitality he would like to accept our hospitality and accompany us to the Wullar 'in your kitchen-boat for a change, because,' he said, 'I am tired of this grand style in which I have to live, and would like to be one of you.'

We were so bounden to the Nawab Zaffar Ullah, as the worthy was called, for the many favours he had heaped on us that we naturally could not refuse him, even though he became more patronizing and added that not only would he like to come with us, but two of his most intimate friends would like to accompany us also, and that he would like to supply provisions and order extra boatmen for our service on the way.

We were in for it, and we accepted all his offers because it would have been more strenuous to find excuses than to let ourselves become completely ineffectual pawns in his high hands. And, accompanied by him and his friends (a surly little judge of the High Court of Kashmir, and a most superficial young trader in hides and skins), we started one evening.

The shades of night were falling and we floated through the heaven and the earth in a dream as yet slightly disturbed by the Nawab and his companions.

The river flowed, and our boat flowed with it, without much help from our boatman, his wife, his sister, or his little daughter.

But we had hardly retired to the silent places of our heart when dinner was announced.

The Nawab had brought a sumptuous meal prepared by his servants already to be served — rice coloured and scented with saffron, curried fowls perfumed with musk, and there were goblets of champagne, bottled in 1889.

Having compromised us into accepting his delicious food, it was only natural that the Nawab should deem it fit to amuse us with the gifts of his speech. He told a few dirty stories and then launched into a discourse of which the ribaldry was so highly spiced with a deliberate obscenity that whoever felt nauseated or not, I, at least, who have never been over-righteous, turned aside, thought of the pride of my emotions, made my words the stars and surrendered myself to the bosom of the night.

When we awoke at dawn our boat had unbarred the floodgates and glided into a veritable ocean of light. For, as far as I could see, for miles and miles, the azure waters of the Wullar spread around us, fluttering a vast expanse of mercury within the borders of the fiery sun-scorched hills.

The Nawab sought to entertain us with a song. But his voice was cracked and only his two friends sat appreciatively acclaiming his genius, while we wandered off to different points of the boat, helping with the cooking, dressing or lazily contemplating the wizardry by which nature had written a poem of broken glass, crumbling earth and blue-red fire.

For, truly, the Wullar is a magnificent spectacle under the red sky at morning.

I gazed upon the placid plain of water spellbound, enchanted. I lent myself to the whispers of the rippling breeze that was awakening the sleepy lotuses: tempted by an unbearable desire to be one with it, I plunged headlong into its midst and bathed in it to my heart's desire. Then I sat, sedulously noticing the blandishments of the elements from the shadow of a canopy under which the Nawab and his friends played cut-throat bridge.

By ten o'clock we had crossed the lake to Bandipur, a dull, insignificant little village on the road to Gilgit, the last stronghold of British Indian power before the earth ventures out into the deserts of Central Asia, uncharted except by shepherds till Soviets brought steel plough of prosperity there.

The Nawab here ordered the *tehsildar* to bring him ten chickens, five dozen eggs and some fruit for our delectation. And he took us about to the dirty houses of the village to show us off, or rather to show himself off, to the poor inhabitants of the township. Our boatman came running and said that we should hurry because he wanted to row us across the middle of the lake before noon, as a squall generally arose in the Wullar every day at noon and it was likely to upset the boat if the vessel hadn't already crossed the danger zone before midday.

The Nawab abused him in Kashmiri, a language in which curses seem more potent than prayers.

We pressed the boatman's point, and since His Grace could not swear at us, he said he would get a man on *begar* (forced labour) to help the boatman and his family to row across the lake more quickly, and he tarried.

The boatman came again after half an hour and found us all waiting impatiently for the Nawab's return from a visit to the lavatory: His Grace had suddenly thought it fit to have a hair cut and a Turkish bath in a *hamam*, and he didn't care what happened to us. When he did emerge from his ablutions, and heard not only the insistent appeals of the boatman, but our urgent recommendations, he, as a mark of his favour, clemency, or whatever you may call it, forthwith stopped a young man of the village who was walking along the cobbled high street and ordered him to proceed to our boat and help to row it to Srinagar.

'But Srinagar is fifty miles away, Sir,' said the young man, 'and my mother has died. I am on the way to attend to her funeral.'

87

'Swine, dare you refuse?' snarled the Nawab. 'You are a liar!'

'No, Nawab Sahib,' said the man, joining his hands. 'You are like God in mercy and goodness. Please, forgive me. I am footsore and weary after a twenty-mile march in the mountains where I went to fetch my uncle's donkey. And now my mother had died and I must see the Mullah about securing a place for her burial.

'Run, run towards the boat,' bawled the Nawab, 'or I'll have you flogged by the *thanedar*. Do you not know that this is the kingdom of which I am a nobleman. And you can't refuse to do *begar*.'

'But, Sarkar...' murmured the young Kashmiri, his lips trembling with the burden of a protest which could not deliver itself in the Nawab's face, which glistened not only with the aura of light that the barber's massage had produced but with the anger which the man's disobedience had called forth.

'Go to the boat, son of an ass!' shouted the Nawab and raised his hand.

At the mere suggestion of the Nawab's threat to strike, the young man began to cry, a cry which seemed childish and ridiculous in so grown-up a person, particularly because there were no tears in his large, brown, wide-awake eyes. And he moaned: 'Oh, my mother! Oh, my mother!' mechanically, in a voice which seemed to express more the cowardice of the Kashmiri which has been bred by the oppression of one brutal conqueror after another, than his very own real hurt.

But the Nawab was too thick-skinned to see the hurt in the man's soul. He looked at the big eyes weeping without tears and heard the shrill crescendo of his cry, and began to laugh.

'Let us leave him, Nawab Sahib,' we said. 'We will give the boatman a hand and row across the lake to safety if we hurry.'

'Wait, wait,' the Nawab said, as he caught hold of the man by his left ear and, laughing, dragged him towards the boat.

The *begari*, who had begun to cry at the mere suggestion of a threat, howled the heavens down at the actual impact of the Nawab's hand on his body, while the Nawab, who had only laughed derisively at first, now chuckled with a hoarse laughter which flushed his cheeks.

The man extricated his ear from the Nawab's grasp as we were about five yards from the boat, and, perhaps because he thought he had annoyed His Grace by so overt an act of disobedience, he knelt down at his feet and, still weeping and moaning, joined his hands and began to draw lines on the earth with his nose as a sort of penance for his sin.

At this the Nawab burst into redoubled laughter, so that his face, his body itself, seemed to swell to gigantic proportions and tower above us all.

'Look!' he said, flourishing his hands histrionically without interrupting his laughter.

But the situation which had been tense enough before had become very awkward now as the man grovelled in the dust and rolled about, weeping, wailing, whining and moaning and sobbing hysterically with the most abject humility.

'Don't you weep, don't you moan, fool!' said the Nawab, screwing his eyes which were full of the tears of laughter, and he turned to the boatman, saying: 'Lift the clown from there and put him on the boat.'

The boatman obeyed the commands of the Nawab, and His Grace having stepped up to the deck behind the *begari*, we solemnly boarded the vessel.

The *begari* had now presumably half decided to do the work, as, crying his hollow cry and moaning his weird moan, he spat on his hands and took up the oar.

The Nawab, who cast the shadow of his menacing presence on the man, was more amused than ever, and he laughed hysterically, writhing and rumbling so that his two friends caught him in their grasp and laid him to rest under the canopy. He sought to shake them off with the weight of his belly and with the wild flourishing of his hands and the reverberating groans of his speech which came from his round red cheeks, muffled with continuous laughter.

The boat began to move, and as the heart-shaped oars tore the water aside, the *begari*, ceased to cry and grieve with the same suddenness with which he had begun.

'Look!' the Nawab bellowed, his hysterical laughing fit ending in a jerky cough which convulsed him as a spark of lightning shakes a cloud with thunder. 'Look!' he spluttered and pointed towards the *begari*.

But the balls of his eyes rolled suddenly; his face flushed ghastly red and livid; his throat, twisting like a hemp rope, gave vent to gasping, whistling noises, and his hand fell limp by his side.

We all rushed towards him.

One of his friends had put his hand on the Nawab's heart, another was stroking his back.

A soft gurgle reverberated from the Nawab's mouth. Then there was the echo of a groan and he fell dead. He had been choked by his fit of laughter.

The boat rolled on across the still waters of the Wullar the way it had come, and we sat in the terrible darkness of our minds, utterly silent, till the *begari* began to cry and moan again, 'Oh, my mother! Oh, my mother!'

Lottery
Dedicated to Stefan

*T*here are certain words which so nearly approximate to the basic emotions of the human heart that though they may belong to one language they easily become current in all the others. Lottery is one of those universal words, and its general acceptability is due largely to the bit of the gambler that there is in every human being, to the belief in luck, fate, or accident of chance, of most people in a universe where little is certain. That one person, from among the millions who buy a ticket or a voucher, should receive a sudden windfall from the money contributed by these millions — that is what most human beings desire in this world of grandiose palaces and empty barns.

There was nothing surprising, therefore, in the fact that Kanahiya, the illiterate hillman from Kangra, who was watchman of the Imperial Bank of India, used the word lottery with almost the same frequency as he smoked a cigarette or puffed at his coconut basined hookah. In fact, this was only to be expected, because, having retired from the army with nothing more than the bluff of the exaggerated prestige of sepoyhood, and a pension of three rupees a month, and seeing large sums of money change hands on the counters, or lying in the vaults of the bank, where he had secured a job following demobilization after the last war, he was, in one way or another, constantly aware of money. Full of admiration for the rich cloth and grain merchants who came to deposit their cotton bags of rupees at the bank every day, saluting the sahibs who drove up in big limousines to negotiate deals, their pockets bulging with paper notes, he had independently evolved the prayer: 'Make me rich, make me rich quick, O God, make me rich,' which he hummed in certain secret moments.

The prayer was, of course, never answered, for, as every one knows, money does not fall like manna from heaven; there is not even a cash system in the celestial sphere, only barter.

So after many vain attempts at getting rich quick, by repeating his prayer, Kanahiya suddeny remembered one day that in the holy books which the village priest used to recite every morning there was something to the effect that only those who work or do something to realize the ideal they seek in prayer find their requests in God answered.

Now, he could not become rich quickly by doing very much in the way of business, because he had no capital. And he could not become rich by getting a more lucrative job, because jobs had been as scarce during the past years as phoenixes — which are supposed to elevate one to kingship if they ever pass over one's head. So, tied to his post, on his unmilitary sentry go at the gates of the bank, his double-barrelled gun in his hand, he had sought to find a way to do something to get rich quick.

At last he had ventured very timidly to ask a manager who was going home on leave how white men came to be so rich.

The sahib, giving the watchman a little bakhshish, had laughed and casually said, Kismet, mere luck. On being pressed further by the persistent Kanahiya about the secrets of white men's success, and how he could emulate the example of the Westerners, the Englishman had jocularly said: 'Try a lottery.'

At first Kanahiya had not been able to understand what the manager sahib meant. But then he had asked Babu Radha Krishan, head clerk of the bank. The Babu had explained to him that there was a lottery called the Calcutta Sweep, for which one bought a share in a ticket at the modest price of ten to twenty rupees, and this might bring one a lakh of rupees if the number of one's ticket coincided with the number of the horse in the race run in Vilayat.

Ever since then the word 'lottery' had become a kind of monosyllabic prayer, a watchword, catchword, cliche, phrase, proverb or whatever you would like to call it, on Kanahiya's tongue. He mumbled it to himself in secret moments when no one was looking, specially at bed-time or in the early morning, and he would talk about it to his friends on the least little excuse.

'You know,' he would say to Badri, the coachman of Lala Banarsi Das, who came on a buggy to the bank, 'there is a magical lottery run in *vilayat** by which, if you buy a ticket, or a share in a ticket, you can become a *lakhpati* overnight if you are lucky to have the horse of your number come first in a race.'

'*Aye*, to be sure,' said Badri dubiouly, 'but if it was as easy to become *lakhpatis* by this lottery you speak about then our lalas would sit at home with their wives rather than sweat in their shops in the cloth market.'

---

*England

93

But as his friends were cynical, Kanahiya would talk about lottery to strangers, mostly because he was talking aloud to himself to confirm his own faith in this extraordinary way of making money. Like his friends, however, the strangers dismissed all his talk about the lottery as the vapourings of a gullible fool. And if he invoked the fact that the manager sahib himself had told him to try a lottery, they said that the sahib had been merely pulling his leg. Babu Radha Krishan's confirmation of the sahib's suggestion, and the details about the Calcutta Sweep lottery which the clerk had given him, seemed to his hearers the complicated talk of a half-baked learned man who was a danger to learning as well as to life.

The dream to get rich quick goaded Kanahiya on, however, in spite of every one, especially after he had consulted Babu Radha Krishan again and again about the exact details of the Calcutta Sweep lottery. And to clinch matters, Babu Radha Krishan offered his services as an intermediary to buy him a share in a ticket for twenty rupees.

Kanahiya had been saving up two rupees a month for years and had piled up two hundred or so rupees in the bank in this way. Further, he had himself turned banker to the poor washermen, sweepers and cobblers who lived in the stables of the gentry in Queen's Road, Amritsar, where he himself occupied a room in an outhouse of Babu Radha Krishan's bungalow. He had earned a fair bit of interest on the money he lent out, so that his total fortune was something like three hundred rupees. 'You can well afford to risk twenty rupees on this lottery,' Babu Radha Krishan said to him, 'rather than go on talking about it and asking questions all the time. I know you have lots of money buried somewhere under the earth in several pitchers.'

The miser in Kanahiya made him hesitate, but the gambler in him egged him on, so the Babu settled the matter for him by actually making him buy a share for ten rupees in a ticket for the Calcutta Sweep in which he himself had bought a share.

During the period when the great race was to be run, somewhere in Vilayat, and the result of the stakes was to be declared, Kanahiya's obsession with lottery became a positive mania. He would pester Babu Radha Krishan for news of the result every day; he would stop all the big Lallas to ask them if they knew anything about the Calcutta Sweep; and he even dared to go up to the new manager sahib, the forbidding little Mr Strong with the bald head and the ginger eyebrows, and asked him about the race. As this sahib, who was not given to levity, said that the result would be out soon and that he himself had bought a ticket in the sweep, Kanahiya calmed down a little and waited with characteristic Oriental patience. His faith in the myth of lottery became so solid, indeed, that when he talked about it now to his friends he did so casually, as though it were an institution as solid as the Imperial Bank of India, only varying from this established firm in that it brought a million-fold interest on one's investment rather than the interest of three percent.

At last Babu Radha Krishan called on him at his hovel in the outhouse one day with a newspaper in his hand and said that the result of the lottery had been declared and published and that, unfortunatley, neither he nor Kanahiya had won anything; but that a peasant, a mere yokel in America, had got the lakh of rupees for the first prize and that two English lords had won the second and third prizes.

The bottom seemed to fall out of Kanahiya's world. He seemed to go pale and almost collapsed with disappointment, so that Babu Radha Krishan had to fetch smelling-salts to revive him. Fortunately for Kanahiya it was a Sunday and he did not have to go to work, and he slept the clock round after he had swallowed some medicine which the Babu gave him.

For a few days afterwards he kept to himself and tried to avoid everyone he knew, both at the bank and among the colony of menials in the stables and outhouses of Queen's Road. His only consolation was that he had not been talking about the lottery overmuch for the last few days, because he had been too worried and expectant about the result. And now he hoped that people had forgotten his pet interest and would not ask him what news he had of the lottery and whether he had become a *lakhpati*. As the strain of earning a living kept most of his own circle of friends busy, and none of them could read a paper, none of them asked him any awkward questions. Only the manager sahib jocularly remarked: 'A good salary for honest work is better than speculation, eh, Kanahiya. Specially for poor people like you and I!' Luckily no one else was listening when the sahib said this; and anyhow, if someone had been there, Kanahiya was assured that they wouldn't have known what the talk was about, since the manager had not mentioned the word lottery.

In fact, Kanahiya so hated this word now that he could not even bear to think of it. All he was concerned about was to somehow make good those ten rupees which he had gambled and to try to save a little more money by pulling in his expenses. He forthwith raised the rate of interest he charged on the loans he gave by an *anna* in the rupee and became the careful watchman he had been before the mania for this lottery had taken possesion of him.

But though he made good his losses on the gamble during the next year and was fairly content, the dream of getting rich quick often assailed him at nights. He would see himself as the landlord of his village, strutting about like a peacock in his fields full of corn, or as a rich lala, splendidly clad, promenading in the Kangra valley, eating mangoes and bathing in the river, before going home to a handsome bejewelled wife. He did not take much notice of these nightly aberrations of his soul, but he did feel afraid that never now would he be able to return to his village as a rich man and marry the daughter of Subedar Raghunath Singh, as he could have done if he had become a *lakhpati*.

Hardened, careful and cynical, he resisted all temptations, however, and tried the safe and sure path of success through saving *pice* rather than risking an *anna* to make a rupee. And he evolved a corresponding philosophy to help to live this modest life: 'A Rajah is a Rajah,' he would say, 'a watchman is a watchman, and a washerman is a washerman. So men were born, each in his place. No one should look at another's buttered bread and cultivate envy or greed. All I want is a bed to lie on, food to eat and work to do to keep myself from thinking too much...'

'And a wife to sleep with,' put in Shankar the washerman.

'No, no, I have no use for women,' Kanahiya said. But when he went to bed that night he felt that there was some truth in what Shankar had said. 'No home is complete without a woman,' he said to himself. 'And, to confess the truth, I have always envied Shankar his wife, Sobha, almost as fair as the Memsahib of Mr. Strong, and with a bottom which winks at one with every step she takes.'

She was the kind of woman he wanted; in fact there was no other woman like her, and it was her he wanted, he said in his mind. But how was he to get her? Another man's wife? It seemed impossible!...

Only, as he contemplated the smiling, happy young form of Sobha in his mind, he realized how often he had looked at her with desire. And if, as the holy men said, to look at a woman with desire was tantamount to having had her, then he had already possessed Sobha in a kind of way. So that

97

even if he eloped with her, there would be no question of sin in it; he would be only claiming a woman who was his by all the rights of love. And how could he run away with her? How could he get another job to survive? And what would people think? He was afraid. He must forget all about this and go to sleep.

Kanahiya tried hard to go to sleep that night, but the agitation which possessed him mounted higher and higher in his brain, while he tossed from side to side on his bed and cried: 'God give me sleep!' After the wrestling of various colloquies in his mind, as he was going over the incidents in his life, he recalled disillusioning business of the lottery. A sudden illumination possessed him: he would not himself risk any more gambles of that sort, but he would persuade Shankar to borrow ten rupees from him on the mortgage of his wife Sobha, and as the washerman was unlikely, as he himself had been, to become a *lakhpati*, he would keep Sobha; for Shankar was already heavily in debt to him and would never be able to pay off the mortgage with interest and get his wife back. That plan settled in his mind, Kanahiya slept the sleep of peace during the rest of the night.

When he woke up in the morning he exposed the plot to the rays of the sun above his head, and, lo and behold, Surya could not outstare him or make him feel ashamed. He tested the plan under the cold shower of the copious water that flowed from the lion-mouthed pump by Gagar Mal's serai, and the design in his mind emerged crystal-clear and pure after the bath. He contemplated the world of men and women about him at the end of Queen's Road and no one seemed to point the finger of accusation against him.

On the way to the bank, therefore, he called on Shankar and said:

'Why, *Ohe* Shankar, what about paying me some of the money you owe me. The interest alone has piled up to ten rupees.'

Shankar stood silently by the donkey on whom he was loading bundles of clothes to go and wash at the ghat; he did not know what to say. To be sure, he had borrowed twenty rupees almost five years ago to celebrate the wedding of his younger brother, but he had not been able to save any money in these hard times to pay back the capital or the interest on it. What could he say? At last he spoke:

'*Ache, bhai*, it is early morning and I am going to the ghat, while Sobha is baking bread to take with us. I shall give you an answer tonight and see if I can find a little ornament to sell or pawn to pay off the interest.'

'This is no talk,' said Kanahiya, putting the heat on, 'I want some of that money.'

'But, brother, it is early morning, and we have hardly awakened yet.'

'Son of the donkey, you are making excuses!' shouted Kanahiya. 'I am a watchman, once a sepoy, and I know how to wake you up properly.' And he flourished his musket at the washerman.

'That would only put me to sleep,' Shankar laughed.

'Oh, illegally begotten, I mean business,' Kanahiya threatened.

'*Acha* then, let us discuss business,' said Shankar, holding the donkey's ear in one hand and offering Kanahiya a seat on the string bed with the other.

'Unless you pay me the whole of the money which you owe me, by tonight, I will take you to the court,' said Kanahiya peremptorily.

'He drinks most of his wages away,' said Sobha from the kitchen. 'Now this will teach him a lesson. He should have saved. He didn't even buy me a skirt.'

'Shut up, prostitute!' Shankar said. 'Don't you interfere in men's business.'

'She is right,' said Kanahiya.

'Yes, watchman Kanahiya Sahib, he rows with me when he gets drunk, and even beats me,' Sobha said.

The washerman sank on to the string bed and sat down silent and defeated.

'Answer me!' Kanahiya bawled.

'What can I say?' said Shankar, after a long pause.

'Well, then, I can suggest a solution to you. I will give you ten more rupees —'

'Oh, generous watchman, sahib, he will only drink it,' said Sobha.

'No, he won't do that,' said Kanahiya masterfully. 'I will give him ten more rupees if he mortgages you, Sobha, to me. With ten rupees he can buy a share in a ticket for the lottery and, if he is lucky, he may become a *lakhpati* and claim you back, as well as pay his dues to me. If not, he forfeits you... Those are my final terms.'

'But Maharaj!' cried Sobha.

'Oh, Kanahiya Seth! You never won that lottery, what chance have I?' said Shankar, his hands joined in supplication.

'I tell you, those are my final terms,' said Kanahiya. 'Think them over during the day; in the evening I must have a settlement. Try your luck; you may be luckier than I.'

And, saying this, he stalked away towards the bank.

All day Kanahiya was in a flutter as he contemplated the rounded contours of Sobha's body in his mind, as he thought of her firm breasts and her fair face. She had sided with him clearly, he felt, in the quarrel with Shankar, that she seemed more than willing to be mortgaged to him in spite of her last show of protest. Besides, he could give her a cake of Pears' soap and some electroplated trinkets and win her love. That word lottery, he gratefully thought. Surely there is a magic in it. Only he hoped that Shankar would not be able to raise the money to pay him off during the day. Anyhow, he had some docuents prepared by the *munshi* of the bank to secure his plans to get Sobha.

After the bank closed he hurried to the washerman's house and, flourishing the musket of his gun in his right hand, demanded, in a hissing whisper:

'Why, *ohe* Shankar, what have you decided?'

The washerman stood silently ironing clothes in the dark room which was both laundry and home to him and Sobha.

'Speak!' blared forth Kanahiya.

Shankar stopped ironing, but could not even lift his head to face the moneylender.

'Don't you see that I have made you a fair offer? You may be lucky and the ten rupees lottery share I have bought you may rid you of all financial difficulties.'

But in the boundless misery of Shankar's heart there was no room even for a particle of faith or even a ray of hope. He just sank down on his knees and, with tears in his eyes, begged Kanahiya for a little more grace.

'The seed of a donkey!' Kanahiya roared in a stentorian voice. 'Be a man and take the chance I am offering you!'

'You, asking him to be a man,' Sobha put in. 'You, a sneaking worm who has designed this plot to ensnare me. Go, you are less than a worm, you are a puffed up ox from the

101

hills with your notions of lottery. Have you become a *lakhpati* that you demand me from the man to whom I am married?'

'Sobha!' exclaimed the amazed Kanahiya, the pallor of chagrin on his face. 'But I thought you said you had no use for this drunkard anyhow!'

'Get out of here!' the washerwoman said regally.

'You bitch of all the dogs in the washerwoman's brotherhood!' shouted Kanahiya, lifting his double-barrelled gun. 'Silent, or I will murder you!' And for a moment he simulated the manner of the dacoits in the films made by Malabar Talkies. Turning theatrically to Shankar, he said, 'Here is the ten-rupee share in that lottery ticket I have bought you... And you, Sobha, come, I will make a woman of you!' And he went towards her.

'I will make you into a man if you don't look out and dare to touch me!' Sobha said.

'Come, don't be difficult,' said Kanahiya, wakening to her in the crisis which meant love or despair for him.

Sobha slapped him on the face with a sharp, clear stroke, while Shankar trembled.

The hillman's blood rose to boiling-point at the insult and he lifted Sobha clear from the waist and carried her out, leaving the wailing Shankar behind. The outhouse in which the washerman lived was hidden from public view and no one heard the shrieks of Sobha nor the moans of her husband.

Locking her up in his own room, without bread or water, Kanahiya sat down on a charpai outside, smoking the hubble-bubble even as he trembled to think of the future. He was afraid that Shankar might call the police, or that the neighbours might tell on him and that the whole of his high-handed behaviour might cost him dearly in the end. But he had taken the precaution of forging a paper, transfixing the thumb-mark of Shankar from a previous deed to a new deal in which the washerman had promised to hand over his wife as a mortgage for arrears of debt and a ten-rupee share of the lottery. Sobha had been too outspoken to every one in the neighbourhood to evoke any sympathy, and Shankar, being weak, Kanahiya hoped for the best.

Sobha banged at the door and cried *dohai** for a long time, until, exhausted, she fell asleep.

Kanahiya went in and, placing some sweets by her, locked the room and slept outside.

When Sobha woke up at dawn and found that he had not touched her, but had instead left sweets by her bed, she, who had been a drudge in Shankar's house, weakened towards Kanahiya to some extent. And when he proposed that he would give up his job and elope to the hills with her she did not protest too loudly.

Before anyone was up in the outhouses, and while Shankar had gone to the cantonment to fetch his uncle, who was employed in a regiment and could get a colonel's letter to enforce his demand for the return of his wife from a mere civilian, Kanahiya bundled Sobha into a *yekka*** with a few belongings and caught the dawn train from Amritsar Junction to Pathankot.

Having plied Sobha with all the gifts that he could buy at Pathankot, Kanahiya headed for a village where he knew a friendly sepoy, and there he remained in hiding for a month or two. Sobha yielded to him after a few more sanguinary battles, for cream cakes would soften any poor woman's

---

* Mercy
** A type of small horse-carriage.

heart, and hot milk with jalebies accelerates the process of conquest. Kanahiya had had a letter of resignation written by a *munshi* at Pathankot, and rested and enjoyed himself to his heart's content.

Then, sober, careful man that he was, he thought of ending his holiday and putting his affairs in order. He had about three hundred rupees in cash and a hundred and fifty owing to him from various clients in Amritsar, apart from the money Shankar owed him, of which he had generously thought of making a free gift to the husband in token of his mistress. With five hundred he was told he could buy a new house and a plot of land sufficient to grow two crops a year. But how was he to get his money back from the clients: he would have to go back to Amritsar once again.

He pondered long over the pros and cons of so hazardous a venture. At last, his gun in hand, and his gambler's instinct emergent again, he decided to risk it.

So off he took Sobha to Pathankot by *yekka*, decked in the best hillwoman's finery, and boarded the night train to Amritsar.

Arriving late next morning, he took a tonga and headed straight for Queen's Road. But the tonga-driver found it difficult to negotiate his vehicle into the path which led to the outhouses of the washermen and sweepers, for a vast concourse of menials was gathered together there, drinking and laughing and singing, dressed in the gayest clothes.

Was it the Holi Festival when the washermen were prone to get very excited, or was someone being married, he wondered.

At last he asked the tonga-driver to ask someone what all the jollity was about.

'Why, don't you know?' said the tonga-driver; 'the whole town knows that the washerman, Shankar, has won the share of ten thousand rupees in the lottery. His ticket came third. I thought you were his guests coming here for the celebrations.'

Kanahiya's face fell. He clutched at his heart and nearly fainted.

'Stop!' he ordered the tonga-driver. 'Wait a while.'

And then he turned towards Sobha.

'You can wait or do what you like,' she said, jumping off the tonga. 'I am going back home.'

And before Kanahiya knew where he was, she was running towards the outhouse which was her home. The bird had flown out of his grasp, and, what was more, he could not now, since Shankar had become a rich and influential man, stay in the neighbourhood lest the washerman put the law on him.

'It's all a lottery — life,' said the tonga-driver sympathetically. 'Do you want to get down or do you want to go back? She has gone. If I were you I should cut my losses and depart in peace.'

The tonga-driver had echoed his inmost thoughts. He had played high stakes and lost; he had played low stakes and the consequences were the same. Life was, indeed, a lottery nowadays. He sighed and said:

'Brother, I'll go back to the station and catch the twelve o'clock train.'

The beat of the *dholki* in the outhouse of Shankar and Sobha fell like the strokes of final doom on his heart and he held his head in his hands.

'Come on, be a man,' said the tonga-driver as he looked round after lashing his horse into a canter...

105

Mahadev and Parvati

Dedicated to Dr. H.K. Handoo

*W*here the milk-white Ganga meets the dusky Jamuna are a few islets and sandy beaches on which the Kumbh Fair is held every twelve years. It is one of the most spectacular and enormous congregations in India, attracting to it the devout and the undevout, from every corner of the land, full of the loftiest aspirations, fears and hopes, hungry for the food of the gods, thirsty for the waters of immortality. Preparations for the fair go on months ahead. The Sadhus and ascetics have *Narsinghas** of copper made to blow their greetings across the Himalayas to Lord Siva from whose mouth the River Ganga is supposed to flow. The Brahmin priests rub up the mnemonic verses from the ancient holy books and evolve a more mysterious and magical ritual than that of previous years, for worship with them is like jugglery, the better the trick the bigger the price earned on it. And the people put by more and more money from their earnings to offer it to the holy men and the priests in order to secure easy passports to heaven.

*One of the incarnations of Lord Vishnu.

106

Though the city of Prayag, where the confluence of the Ganga and Jamuna takes place, is a far cry from Colombo in Ceylon*, in the mind of Parvati, the wife of the engineer Mahadev, it had assumed a significance more subtle than that which she could associate with the nearer shrine of Rameshwaram on the Cape Comorin, or even with the historic temple of Madura near Madras. She had found her grasp on the imagination of her husband slipping for some time, and she thought that a pilgrimage to Prayag, where the breath of the male Siva weds the fiery dark Kali, might in some way cast a spell on him. Mahadev himself would rather have gone to the temple of Konark at Jagannath-Puri, for a change of air and to see some of those famous erotic sculptures which are supposed to stir even the most jaded appetites to new fiercenesses of sexual fury. But the power of an Indian woman's persuasive tongue is only second to that of an American.

So off they went to a suburban railway station by Colombo and boarded a train for the north. Originally Tamils from Coconada, they sighed with nostalgia at the first glimpse of India from the small ship which crosses the short channel from Ceylon to the mainland.

And Mahadev would still much rather have gone to Ooty to drink a little beer in the cafés of the hill station and, if possible, to pick up some Englishwoman like those with whom he had had great success as a student in London. Instead, however, he had to stick to the route planned by Parvati, which led along the straight and narrow tracks of the Madras railway. They had two trunks in a second class carriage all to themselves till Nagpur, but after that the throng of pilgrims began to increase and they had to squeeze into

*Now Sri Lanka

107

a corner, sit sweating, soot-covered and heavy-lidded with sleep. By the time they were a few hours' journey from Prayag there was no room in the carriage to throw a *til* seed. What will not men and women endure to hang on to each other!

At last they reached Allahabad Junction on a torrid morning. Mahadev suggested that, in view of the congestion, it was best to stay at the Parsi hotel in the Civil Lines, and to motor over to Prayag a few miles away. Parvati conceded this as she had been pushed about enough by others more grasping after each other, and heaven, than her.

It was with great difficulty that they secured accommodation in Messrs. Dinshaw's English-style guest-house, for other professional men, too, from all parts of India seemed to have been led by their devoted wives, or the pull of their inherited faith, to the Kumbh Fair. And the atmosphere of the ramshackle hotel, with its tawdry Victorian furuiture and pictures of Edward VII, seemed to the mind of the engineer Mahadev, from the slightly more advanced Ceylon, to be alien and inhospitable.

Parvati, who had been born in the house of a rich Tamil merchant in Malaya, and been married to Mahadev because he had found the dowry of two lakhs of rupees accompanying her a sufficient compensation for her lack of physical charm, was more compromising and docile. For she felt she was nearing the moment when she would realize that union with her husband through the influence of the vision of the two rivers meeting which she had built up like a myth in her mind.

Mahadev was feeling sleepy, but he had to look for a taxi if they were ever to get to Prayag to have a dip in the waters of the Sangham before the sun rose too high; and, of course, taxis were non-existent on this auspicious day,

108

having been requisitioned by the grandees and princes, who can always buy their way to heaven. The couple stood on the roadside and waited for a horse-driven *yekka*. But these were chock full of people from the civil lines on the way to Prayag, and the pilgrims from Ceylon waited in vain. At length someone advised them to trudge it by a short cut. They took the advice and set off.

The rising heat of the morning, the dust of the road and the worry of it, all made Mahadev miserable, as like a good Hindu husband, he walked four yards ahead of Parvati, a polo topee on his head, a white linen suit covering his sweating, heavy-limbed body, his feet thumping at an angle of forty-five degrees.

Their steady patience was, however, soon rewarded, because a *yekka* driver picked them up on to his overloaded carriage, even though it was for the exorbitant sum of five rupees a fare for less than five miles.

Soon they were in sight of the River Ganga. And, already, feeling the impact of the cool breeze which rises from its snow-fed waters, Parvati felt her soul bursting with hope like a lotus. Even Mahadev was excited by the sight of the congregation on the river banks, scattered like shining white blossoms among the groves.

Every instant the din of the fair grew louder. And before long they had alighted and were part of the throng. Mahadev did not know if it was the contagion of togetherness which inspired him, but he dragged Parvati forward with great gusto through the crowd, shouting encouragement to her so as to be heard above the babble of men and women praying, talking, above the persistent calls of the hawkers, the obstreperous wailing of the beggars, the ear-splitting whistles of the toy-sellers.

As they penetrated farther, however, the thrill of community seemed to become suffocating, and Mahadev felt as if he would never get out of the clutches of the swarms of beggars — the blind, the deaf, the dumb, the leprous cripples minus an arm or a leg — all clutching for money and droning like wasps.

'Come this way to the river, sahib,' said a white-robed man, the imprint of sandalwood paste on his forehead clearly showing that he was a priest.

Mahadev felt relieved. And soon he and his wife were out of the claustrophobic atmosphere, seated on a platform by their rescuer, who seemed to be the partner of a hefty Brahmin who presided over the ritual of the dip in the confluence of Ganga and Jamuna.

Mahadev, who had travelled a lot and had endless experience of European guides, might have guessed that a tout is a tout, on the banks of the Ganga as well as on the quay at Marseilles, but for the fact that hardly had he and his wife sat down than the head priest took them completely in his charge and began to weave a fantastic web of mumbo-jumbo verses around the couple's heads, breaking the sacred word into their ears, touching their noses, their chins, and sprinkling the ash of thump on their bodies.

The couple did not speak Hindustani and the priests did not know Tamil or English, except for the tout who spoke a few words of broken Angrezi, but the language of gesture always becomes very potent in such circumstances.

After a lot of spell-binding, the tout tied the end of the loin-cloth Mahadev had assumed with the dhoti of Parvati, having, it seemed, understood the peculiar reason for the couple's pilgrimage. And he led them to the river.

Amid the chants of the holy men, devout worshippers of the Sun, and the hissing prayers of the other men and women themselves, Mahadev and Parvati soaked themselves thoroughly in the water on the spot where the Ganga and Jamuna become one, and dripping, emerged, the ends of their wet clothes still tied together.

The tout led them back to the platform, where the high priest greeted them with more hymns and verses, even as he scattered rice over their heads and made them smell the smoke of sandalwood.

Mahadev and Parvati were by now on the way to being hypnotized into the feeling of togetherness, which they had come here to realize. And, beaming with warm smiles, they stood with joined hands before the agent of God, waiting for the union of their two minds which they felt sure was approaching steadily as the ceremonial became more and more intricate. Parvati was praying in Tamil that she hoped that as Ganga is united with Jamuna, her lord and master would remain united with her and that they would return here together in twenty years.

Suddenly, however, the high priest made a sign as if he was testing a silver rupee on the thumb and forefinger of his right hand.

Through his bleary, half-asleep eyes Mahadev saw it, but did not take any notice.

The high priest repeated the sign and lifted the ten fingers of his hands and said: '*Hazoor*!'

Mahadev was used to being addressed as *Hazoor* and stood with his head upright like a lord of the earth.

At this the tout ducked his head forward before Mahadev's gaze and said, in broken English: 'Rupee one thousand!' And thrusting his palm forward said: 'Give.'

111

Mahadev opened his eyes wide with astonishment and incomprehension.

'One thousand, charge for ceremony! Understand? Give now!'

The tout's words were like hammer blows.

Mahadev swept his wife's face with a sharp glance and then, blinking his eyes, he waved his head, saying: 'No.'

'Put money here,' the tout said, rapping his knuckles on the platform.

Parvati nudged her husband to goad him to render forth unto God the price of His acceptance of her prayer, though she had no idea how much God was demanding.

In order not to give her the impression that he was being mingy or mean over the offerings, Mahadev joined his hands meekly to both the priest's and said: 'Fifty rupees.'

'How much does he say?' the old priest asked the tout.

The tout told him in Hindustani. Whereupon the high priest poured out a flood of Sanskrit imprecations asking the Gods to come and witness the impudence of the couple. And the tout shouted at Mahadev in a mixture of English, Hindustani and Punjabi, a great deal about how these dirty, beef-eating southerners come and want to expiate their sins by offering a few pieces to the servants of God...

'One hundred rupees!' Mahadev offered generously to avoid the fuss.

The tout caught hold of the knot on the *dhotis* of the couple and began to sever it.

Parvati turned and saw the symbol of her togetherness with her husband in danger of being destroyed. She began to weep, and caught hold of Mahadev's arm with tender, supplicating hands.

Mahadev patted her on the head even as he addressed the tout in English and appealed to him to be a gentleman.

'Give a thousand rupees at once! Or I will break your head!' the tout answered. And he flashed his red eyeballs menacingly at the engineer.

The high priest added his quota of bullying and remonstrance.

A crowd began to gather together, muttering all kinds of malicious and unfriendly sentiments about southerners.

Mahadev felt the same claustrophobia now as he had experienced on his arrival at the fair. With a pitiful sob he put his head on his joined hands and knelt before the high priest, begging to be excused and offering two hundred rupees.

The high priest dismissed his abject apology with the most perfunctory of godly gestures.

And the tout, feeling that he had broken the pilgrim's will, struck Mahadev on the head, saying: 'Get up. You won't escape this way. A thousand rupees and no less!'

'Oh, don't be so cruel,' said a kindly pilgrim, coming to Mahadev's help. 'He is a stranger in these parts.'

'Go, go your way, and leave our votary,' the tout answered.

Weeping huge tears which fell on his chubby cheeks, Mahadev pulled Parvati near him and then explored for his wallet in the pocket of the shirt he had left behind before going to dip in the Sangham. It was not there. He looked furiously in the other pocket. No, he recalled he had put it in the pocket he had searched first. Panic stricken, he took up his trousers and dug his hands into its two pockets. There was no sign of the wallet. The pallor of death spread on his face and he turned towards the high priest and the tout, now angrily, accusingly.

'A thousand rupees!' the tout said.

'You have stolen my money!' Mahadev shouted. 'Give me my wallet or I will call the police!'

'The thief threatening the sheriff!' the tout said to the crowd and raised his hand to strike Mahadev.

Parvati was weeping hysterically now. The ceremony of her innocent desire had been drowned in this vulgar brawl.

Mahadev looked at the two priests helplessly and, with a sudden loathing that would not transgress the code of good manners he had learnt, he surveyed the crowd for the figure of a policeman. There seemed none within reach.

'If you want to spare yourself more trouble at their hands, sir, please go away,' a well-spoken pilgrim suggested.

Mahadev picked up his clothes and, putting his arm round Parvati, moved away. He had never felt so near her before...

Eagles and Pigeons

*F*rom Mishtar Ghulam Mustafa, resident at 2 King's Lane, off Paradise Street, Libpool, this letter is sent to his father, Chaudhri Ahmed Din, peon Canal Department, Village Kanowan, Tehsil Gurdaspur, District Gurdaspur.

After salaams and respects to my mother, I have to say that by the grace of Allah I have reached Libpool safely, and I hasten to write to you because you may not read about my safety in the newspapers; in the Angrezi newspapers the names of only sahib seamen, who have died or survived from pop-guns, bombs and torpedoes, are written and not the names of native seamen and Lascars; and I don't know if the Hindustani newspapers have any news of what is going on in these parts. Respected father, ask my mother not to be frightened if she learns that I have been saved from death, saved just when the Angel of Death, Israel, flew over like an eagle and dropped bombs and sank the vessel in which I had been working. Twelve sahibs and twenty-three Hindustani seamen dived into the sea forever, and I swam for four hours in the icy sea before a boat which was truly like Hazrat Noah's Ark picked me up. As you know, I always laughed at the Mullah for saying everything was ordained by God, and mocked at my mother for believing in Fate, and I still don't believe in either, but I tell you one thing — the moment when Life meets Death is frightening.

It all happened in this way. One day I was riding a bicycle — do not be amazed, but I learnt to ride the steel horse in an hour; it is simple. An imposing *afsar*, a second mate sahib from his uniform, stopped me at the door of the docks and asked me if I wanted a boat. This was good luck, for I had not had a boat for four months and in famine times brackish water is sweet.

I told the sahib the time of my service on Angrezi ships, which is now two years and three months out of the four since I left home.

The second mate sahib said: 'If you want a job as a deckan I will fix you on an oil tanker running from here to Africa — six pounds a month and food-lodging.'

I had never before been on such a ship. By the rules of the Angrezi Sarkar we Hindustani seamen are only employed on ships carrying cargo, species of boats for carrying goods as there are species of goods trains.

I signed on and was paid some money in advance, most of which I sent you — I hope you got it in time to pay the mortgage on our holding.

The calf's teeth seemed golden, so I came home and told some other Hindustani brothers who had been without jobs for one full moon to another for three months. And they too went and signed on. We said to ourselves we will go and see new lands and have some experience. How could we know, Father, that the Eagles would swoop down on us and that we Pigeons would flutter and, leaving half to seek the whole, some of us would drown without finding bottom.

But there is a war on in these parts and no one knows much nowadays because the sea is alive with electricity and the sky is replete with thunder and the wonder is that I am alive to tell the tale.

Perhaps it was the *Captan* Sahib of the ship who was to blame. We were two days out at sea and never saw him on deck.

The steward sahib was kind, however, and told me not to be frightened of the noises, as, he said, the skipper (which means the *Captan* in Angrezi) is a gentleman, though he is fond of the bottle and hard on the crew as a spider on the flies.

Our sleeping quarters were better than on other ships: the bed-mats were full of cotton instead of straw, and we had two blankets each and there were no fleas, though there were some bugs and cockroaches. But we did not trouble about them, for to eat the food of beggary is to warm yourself at the fire of chaff and the bread of work is alone honourable — though it is work and sleep for a sailor, more work than sleep!

When we touched port and the oil was emptied we had to go down to the tanks with buckets and cloths and clean them out. The smell is similar to that in Rahmat's oilmill, Father, and it gives one a headache, besides stirring the bile. I kept some black pepper seeds in my mouth which Hakeem Hasham Ali used to prescribe for sickness and I fared well. And we were given a ration of rum to put more life into us after we had cleaned the tanks, for it was cold work. And all was well until the calamity visited us which was to visit us.

We were on our way back in an angry sea. And, suddenly, before we knew where we were, a steel bird flew over us.

The third mate aimed a pop-gun and fired at the bird as it swooped down on us like the eagle which snatched the fried bread out of my hand when I was a child.

The eagle's excrement is said to spread leprosy whenever it falls. The filth which this steel bird excreted, and which at first fell in the sea, spread a poisonous smoke all over us.

For a while this raider from the skies made off and we breathed freely, though no one could feign a sleep-walk after the shock it gave us.

The *Captan*, the first, second and the third mate were all running in a confusion.

Some of the seamen and I touched our ears.

But before we had turned to look, *lo*! the raider had sent a bigger steel bird, as if the first little angel disguised as an eagle had just come to announce our doom and then Hazrat Israel himself had appeared, disguised as a bigger eagle, to drown us in the deluge.

The Angel of Death roared across our ship, hovered round it, turned tail and returned again and again, dropping bombs and scattering bullets, till the tanker became a cauldron in which life was being roasted like grain.

The first, the second, and the third mate fired back with pop-guns, but a few pulses will not burst the stars, and the angel of annihilation had done his work: our ship was on fire and so were our blistering hearts and smoky clay.

I was standing beside our bo'sun, who was wounded on the deck. I tied a piece of my long shirt on his arm and chest. But, Father, truly he was a brave man. He did not moan or

118

speak, only he could not help the tears in his eyes. I asked him whether he was badly wounded. He shook his head, but he said he had been married only a month and his wife would be sad to know he was dead. The Angrezi seamen, too, Father, have the same hearts as us folk. In fact, they love their women more openly. Don't think I am shameless, or have turned a Christian, but while we Hindustanis beat about the bush the Europeans catch the bird.

The ship was sinking and the crew was jumping overboard.

I lifted the bo'sun and flung him near a boat and then jumped off myself. But when I looked round in the water I could not see him. And from now on each one fought for his own life and for those immediately near him.

I swam and swam and swam until my body was numb with cold and stiff. I remembered Mother, not because I didn't think of you, but because her name comes to me every time I am in danger, and I almost gave up, only straining to keep afloat, thinking in one breath there are a thousand breaths.

And then, wonder of wonders, a ship came towards us. It had got a message from a brave man on our ship who had struck out the telephone without wires in all directions before he had been killed.

Only seventeen of us were picked up, Father, and today there is darkness in many homes. But I tell you that it is just chance that I am alive and sit here in the café sipping tea and writing to you a letter from my grateful heart.

You used to say that the ways of God are strange, but truly the ways of man are stranger. If a man slays another man in a street he is a murderer and is hung by the law courts, but if one Sarkar fights another there is no one to do justice between them. Some dacoits, highwaymen and murderers, who started by looting other people's land, have set the

119

world on fire, so that the whole earth has become a funeral pyre. The smoke of war has spread far and wide and everywhere there is darkness, relieved only by the dim light of hope in men's eyes. Oh, it is a mad world, Father! The robbers have pitted brother against brother, kinsman against kinsman. And they have heaped treachery, murder, lies, on one another like the debt on our family.

No one calls his own curds spoiled, but even some of the seamen sahibs say that they have done many things to our country which are wrong and that we brother seamen will join hands and all wrongs shall be righted.

But our victory is in our own hands, Father, and we have to unite and work for it, with steel courage and iron determination. For freedom does not fall like manna from heaven; it is born of struggle without fear.

Acha, if our own Raj comes I hope all debts will be cancelled, so that I can return home, for farming is best, trades next, service is poverty, and beggary worst of all.

Again with my respectful salaams to you and my mother, and pats on the heads of my brothers and sisters, I am your son,

GHULAM MUSTAFA

❑❑❑